TALES OF THE TOWPATH
ADVENTURES ALONG
THE LEHIGH & DELAWARE CANALS

Written By Dennis Scholl

Illustrated By Dennis Gerhart

First published in the United States of America in 2009 by Delaware & Lehigh National Heritage Corridor, Inc. Fourth printing, September 2016.

For information about permission to reproduce selections from this book, write:
Permissions, Delaware & Lehigh National Heritage Corridor
2750 Hugh Moore Park Road, Easton, PA 18042

ISBN: 9780974294421
Library of Congress Control Number: 20009902043

Book design by Anne Schauer, Saraceno Design Inc., Bethlehem, PA
Christmas City Printing Company, Inc., Bethlehem, PA

Visit the Delaware & Lehigh National Heritage Corridor, Inc. online at: www.delawareandlehigh.org.
Visit the *Tales of the Towpath* website online at: www.delawareandlehigh.org/talesofthetowpath.

INTRODUCTION

Tales of the Towpath is a story about growth and change: the industrialization of the United States; a family struggling to prosper in a new land; the maturing of an inquisitive young boy who meets new friends and enjoys exciting adventures that shape his life.

Finn Gorman is the curious son of Fergus Gorman, a hard-working Irish immigrant who brings his family to America in 1846. The Gormans arrive as America is entering a new age of prosperity. Enterprising men are creating new industries that change the way people work and live. New forms of transportation are opening the American frontier to settlement. Abundant forests are supplying lumber for all the needs of a growing country. Farms from New England to the Deep South feed a population that grows every day.

In the middle of this prosperity are the country's canals. They are the superhighways of the time; long, narrow waterways that connect towns and cities across much of the United States. Boats that navigate them carry coal, building materials, manufactured goods and farm products. Fergus Gorman becomes part of the booming canal life when he launches a boat on the Lehigh and Delaware canals in 1855. His business is a family effort.

Finn Gorman's memorable adventures along the canals introduce him to people and places that played important roles in this time of growth and change known as the American Industrial Revolution. Travels with his father help Finn grow up. He learns that life on the canals can be unpredictable, exciting and mysterious…and always full of important lessons.

CHAPTER 1

FINN'S MYSTICAL MOMENT

My father was a very wise man, one of those people who is always right no matter what the situation. He used to tell me that everyone experiences a day when they relive events of the past, exactly the way they happened the first time. I never understood how Father knew something like that. Today I finally learned what he meant.

Maybe it was the hot sun or maybe I was just extra tired, but something I can't describe stopped me during my afternoon walk along the Lehigh Canal in Freemansburg, where I've lived most of my eighty-five years. A sensation unlike anything I felt before pulled me to the edge of the canal and compelled me to gaze into its still, green water. I felt like a moth being drawn to a flame.

I didn't see anything unusual. My reflection was the same one that I saw in my bedroom mirror every morning: an old man with gray hair, gray moustache, a wrinkled face, and a pair of old, worn, gold-rimmed glasses on the tip of his nose. I chuckled to myself, thinking how the passing of time had changed me.

I felt I needed a closer look at the reflection, so I bent down on my hands and knees and stared into the water. I noticed something different about my eyes. They didn't look like the same pair I had seen in the mirror a few hours before.

These eyes were wide – really wide – and they seemed to smile with a child's wonder. They looked like my eyes when I was a boy. I didn't know what was happening. It was absolutely silly, but I reasoned the only way I'd get to the bottom of this was to talk to the reflection. Oddly enough, the reflection looked like it wanted to talk to me, too. I stared and stared at the water. Who was going to say the first word? I finally got the nerve to open my mouth.

"Finn Gorman," I whispered, hoping no one was watching or listening. "Is that you?"

There was no response. I leaned a little closer and whispered again.

"Well, of course I know it's you, or should I say me? I recognize the moustache and glasses. But whose eyes are those, and why do they look so different than they did this morning?"

Those two bright eyes widened more and more with each question I asked. They sparkled and twinkled like heavenly stars on a dark summer night. It was as though they had ears and a mind of their own.

"Finn Gorman, there's still a boy in me, isn't there?"

The reflection was silent. I persisted.

"I know I'm old," I admitted, "I know I can't run and jump or swim in the canal. But I've still got a boy inside me, don't I? Please tell me you're there, young Finn."

A swift wind suddenly blew over the canal and broke the stillness of the water. My smiling reflection turned into a shimmering shape that spread in all directions and finally disappeared. I watched it fade and closed my eyes, disappointed that young Finn was gone.

Then the wind stopped just as quickly as it started. The sound of the nearby steel factories and railroad yards faded. The air had an eerie silence. I looked down at the water again, hoping I'd see what was there before.

To my utter amazement, a boy was staring back at me, a boy with no wrinkles or gray moustache or glasses. This boy had smooth, fair skin, a head full of bushy brown hair, and a smile as wide as a crescent moon.

I beamed as I had never beamed in my life, and the boy in the water looked straight at me and beamed right back. I knew this was the day my father had told me about. I closed my eyes and clutched the stone I had worn around my neck for so many years. Then I waited for whatever was in store for me, knowing I would not be disappointed.

CHAPTER 2
A FAMILIAR PLACE

I didn't know where I'd be when I opened my eyes, but I hoped it wasn't Freemansburg. I always dreamed of trapping beaver in the Rocky Mountains or hunting buffalo and antelope on the great grass plains of Kansas, but I never got there. After so many years living in one place, I truly hoped for a change of scenery.

I summoned my courage and slowly opened my eyes. I was in a strange yet familiar place, with sights and sounds I had seen and heard before. I felt like I was dreaming, yet everything in front of me was alive and moving. There were teams of mules pulling canal boats filled with shiny black coal and big sacks of flour. Behind me was a broad, swift-flowing river with a small, neatly arranged town built along one of its banks.

I remembered this place. I remembered this life. My heart beat faster than it ever had in the past fifty years. I wondered if my father was right. Was this the day when I would relive my life's most important events?

"Look out, boy!" a man shouted. "Can't you see the mules coming? Get off the towpath before you're trampled."

"Yes, sir," I called back, quickly moving to the side. "I'll get off the towpath right away."

The man's warning echoed through my mind. Did he call me a boy? Why, I was older than him by half a century. I moved away from the towpath and took off my hat to wipe the sweat from my forehead. When my hand passed my eyes, I stopped it dead still and took a long look. Was this *my* hand? The skin was smooth and fair; not a single wrinkle. Then I looked down. What happened to the gold-rimmed glasses on the tip of my nose? And where was my gray moustache? Good gracious! My reflection wasn't lying. I *was* a boy!

I grabbed for my stone, but it was gone.

"Finn!" someone shouted in the distance. "Finn Gorman, where are you?"

I looked toward the voice and saw a tall man waving. He was standing next to a building with a big sign that read "Freemansburg Boat Livery."

Freemansburg? This couldn't be Freemansburg, at least not the same Freemansburg where I woke up this morning.

I waved back, but didn't know to whom I was waving.

"Come here, Finn," the man shouted again. "We've got work to do."

Suddenly, I remembered the man's voice. It was the same voice that had taught and comforted me when I was a boy. My eyes became wet with tears. I started running toward the boat livery. It seemed as though my legs couldn't carry me fast enough.

"Father, I'm coming!" I yelled to the man. "Wait for me!"

Good heavens, I *was* in Freemansburg, and right now it was the most exciting place on earth. Somehow I had become ten years old again. Was I in a fantasy, or was this real?

"Finn!" Father yelled again.

The voice was no fantasy. Whatever happened had brought me back to a man I loved and missed.

COMING TO AMERICA

As I ran down the towpath, I remembered Father's story of how we came to Freemansburg. It was a story worth repeating.

My father and mother – Fergus and Mary Gorman – came to America from Ireland, where they had lived in a seaport called Belfast along the Irish coast. Father was a carpenter who built sailing ships. Mother took care of her family and sewed clothing for extra income.

I was born in 1845, four years after my brother, Colin. In 1846, Father and many other people were forced to leave Ireland because they were starving. Irish people depended on growing potatoes for food and money, but the country's potato crop became diseased and rotted in the ground. People all over Ireland were left without food. Many of them became sick and died. Father called it a famine.

The shipyard where Father worked went bankrupt during the potato famine and Father lost his job. He loved Ireland, but with no job and a growing family, the only thing he could do was find a better place to live. Father heard about a country on the other side of the Atlantic Ocean called America. People said it was a "land of opportunity," a place where you could live your dreams. A big city called New York was supposed to be a good place to start.

Father used most of his savings to buy tickets for the ship that sailed to America. Colin remembers how packed the ship was with passengers, and how sick so many of them became from the rough sea. There was hardly any space to sleep. Mother and Father never said much about the trip; I don't think they liked it.

We arrived in New York with hundreds of other people from Ireland, Scotland, and Wales. We survived on the streets until Father was hired as a carpenter at a huge shipyard. His pay was enough to rent a small room in a crowded tenement house. Mother began sewing for the

landlord's family, which brought in a few extra dollars. However, we still had very little money.

Our room was on the third floor of the building. We lived, slept, cooked and ate there. A small stove heated our food and kept us warm. When we wanted water, we had to go to an outside pump. Everyone used it. When we needed a toilet, we went outside and stood in line at a little shack called a "privy." Everyone used that, too.

We lived in the tenement house for almost two years. There was always a threat of fire, and Mother worried about gangs on the streets. When Father wasn't working, he spent his time in our room helping Mother take care of Colin and me. He often said he felt like a rat trapped in a tin can.

Workers at the ship docks talked about getting out of New York. Some of them heard of a place called Pennsylvania. There were jobs there building canal boats. That appealed to Father. He heard that if you saved enough money, you could buy a canal boat and be your own boss. That sounded even better. From that point on, it became Father's plan.

WAGON HO!

My legs finally got me to the Freemansburg Boat Livery. I was nearly out of breath. "Finn, I've never seen you run so fast," Father told me. "And you're so pale. You look like you've just seen a ghost."

Looking around me, I felt like I *was* seeing ghosts. First I saw Mr. Steckel, the saddle maker, and then Mrs. Freeman, the doctor's wife. Teddy Bachman was helping his father at the coal yard. Jennie Geissinger was walking along the towpath. I was always a little sweet on her. I pinched myself to make certain I wasn't dreaming. Ouch! Sure enough, I was awake.

"Finn, we have a lot to do before we leave on our trip," Father told me. "Conan is at the stable getting a new shoe. Here's twenty-five cents to pay Mr. Ritter, the blacksmith. Please give it to him and then walk Conan to the house."

Conan? I'd be happy to get Conan. Why, I hadn't seen that old mule in more than seventy years. He was a special animal, bigger and stronger than a horse and much smarter. That's why Father named him Conan, which means "wisdom"

in the old Irish language.

Conan entered our life the day we left New York in the spring of 1848. I never understood how Father saved enough money to buy a mule and a wagon, considering the little pay he earned at the shipyard, but he made a good purchase. We could not have left the city without Conan pulling us and all our belongings.

Colin was seven years old when we moved. He loved to tell stories about the trip. He recalled how the roads we followed in New Jersey were narrow and made of dirt. There were rocks that stuck up everywhere and made the ride very bumpy. Colin said that one time the wagon got jarred so hard that he tumbled out and landed on something stinky that Conan just deposited on the road. Yech! I laughed every time he told me that story.

It took four days to travel through New Jersey. Before we could enter Pennsylvania we had to cross the Delaware River. It was wide and deep. When we arrived at the river's edge, Father coaxed Conan to pull the wagon onto a long raft called a ferry. It was connected to a thick wire cable that stretched from shore to shore. Once we were on, the operator took some money from Father and slowly floated us across the river. Colin says he prayed until we got to the other side.

Mother remembers how Father's face shined when we got off the ferry and drove the wagon up a hill overlooking a city called Easton. He could see two canals: One stretched to the west and followed a smaller river called the Lehigh; the other followed the broad Delaware to the south. Each canal was full of boats.

"Mary," Father told Mother as he pointed to the scene below the hill, "someday you and I are going to own a boat like one of those. It will bring us a good life."

Our journey from Easton continued along a road that followed the Lehigh River. Conan pulled us up and down hills for miles. We finally arrived at a long bridge that crossed the river. It was covered with a wooden roof and sides. Colin remembers thinking it was a tunnel made of wood. Father whistled to Conan and the big mule pulled us inside.

On the other side of the bridge was a sign that read "Welcome to Freemansburg." One of the canals we had seen in Easton was there, too. It was very busy. People operating the boats on the canal – men *and* women – were very busy, too. But they had satisfied looks on their faces, very much unlike the frowns people wore in New York. Mother knew by the smile on Father's face that this is where we would settle. There was no city smoke, no foul odors and no crowded tenement buildings.

Father found a room to rent that was small but comfortable. He needed money to pay the landlord, so he sold the wagon. But he would not sell Conan, even though the mule would have fetched a good price. Conan was an important part of Father's plan. He stayed in town at a mule stable, which Father cleaned without pay in exchange for Conan's food and a stall. Conan seemed happy there with all his mule friends.

Mother often said it was good fortune that led us to Freemansburg. In just a few days, Father had a job building canal boats. He learned how to build them, steer them, and load them so the weight of the cargo was evenly balanced. He also learned how to fix them when they needed repairs. In short, Father learned everything about canal boats that there was to learn.

His plan was working.

CHAPTER 5
BUILDING A FUTURE

"Finn, did you forget something?" I looked up. It was Mr. Ritter the blacksmith. "Did your father give you money for Conan's new shoe?" he asked.

"Oh, I'm sorry, Mr. Ritter," I stammered. "My mind was somewhere else."

I reached into my pocket and handed Mr. Ritter the twenty-five cents. Conan seemed pleased with his new shoe. I took his reins and walked him across the covered bridge at the end of Main Street.

Our home was on the other side of the Lehigh River, on a hillside overlooking the little village of Shimersville. We moved there when I was seven. By then Father decided our room in Freemansburg was too small for a family of four, and that didn't include the baby Mother was expecting. He saved enough money to buy some land and build a house. He felt Shimersville was a perfect place to live.

The hillside Father chose had a gentle slope, which was good for growing crops. It also had a crystal-clear spring bubbling right out of the

ground. That became our drinking water. The view was hard to beat. We could see Freemansburg and Bethlehem across the river and even had a clear view down the old King's Road into Hellertown.

Colin and I often took walks along the banks of the Lehigh River and Saucon Creek. We heard stories about an Indian village that once stood at Shimersville. That was exciting! I'd search the edge of the water, looking for arrowheads and stone tools. Sometimes I thought I found some, but the other kids said they were just sharp rocks. I wasn't so sure.

Our house was as solid as the hillside. A kind man named Mr. Knecht helped Father build a thick foundation, a fireplace and a chimney, all from large pieces of field stone. Mr. Knecht owned an iron foundry in Shimersville but he always found time to help. He assigned everyone a job. Colin and I gathered rocks from the hillside and lifted them into Mr. Knecht's wagon. Conan pulled the wagon to the house. Mr. Knecht, who was a stone mason as a young man, chose the best rocks and chiseled them into pieces that fit like a puzzle.

Father took over when the stonework was done. He and Colin built a wooden frame for the house from heavy chestnut timbers and thick oak boards. I supplied them with nails and drinking water. Father taught me how to use a hammer, but one time I missed a nail and hammered my thumb. After that, I decided to stick with supplying materials.

Father proclaimed the house fit for living once we had four walls, a roof, and a floor. We moved in and slept on the floor until Father had enough time to build bed frames. In order to save more money, Father learned how to plow fields and plant crops. That way we could grow our own food and Mother could preserve some of it for the winter. Conan wasn't fond of pulling a plow, but eventually he took to it like a fish takes to water. Colin and I followed the plow and picked up overturned rocks. We put them into the wagon and unloaded them at the edge of our land, where we stacked them waist-high in nice, straight rows. They made a perfect fence, one that would last forever.

We used some of the rocks to line the inside of a large hole Father dug next to the house. It became our underground storage for vegetables, fruits and other food that needed to be kept cold, such as eggs and butter and cheese. Father called it a root cellar. He built steps to enter the cellar and a door that we had to bend down to open. On a hot summer day, it was a good place to escape the heat.

Mother was as happy as I had ever seen her. She was in a home for the first time since leaving Ireland. It was her home, bought and paid for. She cooked and made clothes, some that were much too small for Colin and me. I didn't understand why until Mother's belly started growing. Then in late summer, little Rose came along. I wasn't the baby anymore.

CHAPTER 6

THE BELFAST QUEEN

Father never strayed from his plan to own a canal boat. After our house was built, he worked even more hours at the Freemansburg Boat Livery to earn enough money to make his dream come true.

Once a week he hitched Conan to our wagon and took Colin and me to Bethlehem. Our first stop was always at a bank where Father would leave most of his earnings from the boat livery. He said the money would grow at the bank and one day there would be enough to pay for a canal boat. I didn't understand how money grew in a bank, but I knew Father always had a good plan.

One evening at supper, Father said he had an announcement. Colin and I looked at each other wondering what we were about to hear. Mother had a slight smile on her face, but seemed more interested in keeping little Rose off the table than listening to Father's news.

It didn't take long for Father to come to the point.

"I bought a boat," he said, looking very proud and happy. "I bought a fine canal boat that will serve us for many years. It's going to be the start of a new life for all of us."

You could have heard a pin drop. I looked at Colin. His mouth was so wide open that he could have swallowed a duck. Mother was smiling, but quiet. Father looked bewildered. He couldn't understand why someone wasn't saying something.

Finally, Mother broke the silence. "Fergus, I know it was your dream to own a canal boat, and you have worked hard to reach your goal. I am very happy for you, and very proud."

Then Mother turned to Colin and me. "Boys, do you have anything to say?"

We didn't know what to say. We were happy, of course, but what would it mean for us? A new life? Would I see my friends? I gathered the courage to ask a question.

"Father, will we be on the boat with you?"

Father's mouth formed a wide smile. "Of course! I will be the captain and you and Colin will be my crew. Colin will handle the mules and you will be the cook."

A cook? Colin nearly burst out laughing. I felt I should bring something to the captain's attention.

"Father, I can't cook," I said, hoping he would reconsider my assignment. "I don't know anything about it. We'll all starve."

"You'll learn, Finn," Father assured me. "Mother and little Rose won't be joining us on the canal, but your mother is still part of the crew. Her job is to teach you how to cook. Remember, Finn, a crew is only as good as each member. I know you'll become a good cook and help the crew."

"Aye-aye, Captain," I said somewhat reluctantly. "I'll do my best."

"Father," Colin said. "I heard you say mules, but we only have one. Are we getting another?

"Yes, Colin, we are," he replied. "Conan can't pull a boat by himself. He needs help. His partner will be arriving soon."

Colin had another question. "Father, we have a boat, but does it have a name?"

Father and Mother looked at each other. They smiled in a way I had not seen before, a smile that revealed trust and understanding.

"Colin, Finn," he said. "Mother and I have decided to call the boat the *Belfast Queen*, in honor of our home in Ireland and in honor of your mother, the queen of our family."

Colin reached for his cup of water and stood up. He stretched out his arm, raised the cup in the air and cleared his throat to say something.

"I'd like to propose a toast," he said. "I propose a toast to the *Belfast Queen*!"

We smiled and rose to our feet. "To the *Belfast Queen*!" we exclaimed.

Laughter filled the room. Everyone was happy. A new life was about to begin, a life on the canal.

CHAPTER 7

THE GREAT DISCOVERY

While I was learning how to cook in Mother's kitchen, Colin was learning how to handle a mule in the field behind our house. Little did he know that his training would lead to the greatest discovery of my life.

A mule driver and his mules need to understand each other. Father knew that. He felt the best way Colin and Conan could get to know each other was to have them team up and go to work. So, every day Colin put a harness on Conan and hitched him to our plow. Father's plan killed two birds with one stone: He developed a good team to pull our boat and got new crop fields plowed at the same time.

About three weeks before the start of our trip, Father showed up with a surprise that nearly rivaled the announcement of the *Belfast Queen*. Colin and I were in the corn field with Conan when we saw a wagon drive up the hill to our house. Father and Mr. Knecht were in the front seat; hitched to the back was a sassy, dark brown mule. It fussed all the way up the hill, trying to stop the wagon even though

there were two strong horses pulling it.

"Oh, my," Colin said to me. "Looks like I got my second mule. Let's go see him."

We raced down the hill. Conan stayed in the field with the plow, watching all the commotion with great interest. We reached the wagon just as it pulled in front of our house.

"Boys, meet our new mule," Father exclaimed. We examined the animal from head to foot. "What's his name?" Colin asked.

"He doesn't have one yet," Father replied. "That's up to us. Right now this mule needs to meet his partner. Colin, please bring Conan down here."

Conan didn't need any encouragement. He had been eyeing the new mule from the second it arrived. As soon as Colin reached Conan and unhitched the plow from his harness, that old mule bolted down the hillside like lightning from the sky. He ran straight for the new mule. Everyone scattered. Mr. Knecht barely got out of Conan's way.

"Whoa, mule!" Colin kept shouting as he ran down the hill. "WHOA!"

We thought the mules would collide, but Conan dug his front hooves into the ground and stopped abruptly no more than six inches from the new mule's nose. He was taller than this newcomer by an ear. When the two stood next to each other, it was easy to tell which one was in charge.

"Do you think they like each other?" I whispered to Colin.

"I don't know," he answered. "Let's see what they do."

Then Conan let out a sound I never heard before.

"*Hee-awwww!*" the old mule bellowed. Once, twice, three times.

The new mule stood frozen in his tracks. Then he stretched his head toward Conan and made the same "*Hee-awwww*" sound, but not nearly as loud and only once. And that quick, they shot off at a dead run toward the corn field, criss-crossing up the hillside as they went.

"I think they like each other!" Colin shouted to everyone. "I think they're trying to be friends."

Father shook Mr. Knecht's hand and thanked him for helping get the new mule home. That night Conan and his friend stayed in the shed and we gathered at the dinner table to choose the new mule's name. Everyone had ideas but no one could agree.

"Fergus," Mother said at one point in the conversation, "did you see the reddish spot of hair the mule has on its forehead?"

"Yes, I did, Mary," Father replied. "Why do you mention it?"

"I know you named Conan in the old Irish language after someone who is wise," Mother explained. "In old Irish, Rogan means something that's red in color, like our new mule's spot of hair. Do you think Rogan might be a good name for the mule?"

"Rogan," Father thought, rubbing his chin with his fingers. "Rogan. Yes, indeed, Mary, I like it."

And so the spunky mule became Rogan, the newest member of our crew.

Everyone was awake early the next morning. It was time to see how Conan and Rogan worked as a team. Colin and I put the harnesses on them and led them to the corn field. I stepped back once they were hitched to the plow.

Colin snapped the reins. "Go mules!" he shouted. Conan listened and started at his normal pace, but Rogan kicked and tried to break free.

"Whoa, mule! WHOA, MULE!" Colin shouted again and again. But Rogan had no idea what "Whoa, mule!" meant. I watched and silently thanked Father for making me the cook. Finally, Conan put an end to all the excitement.

"*Hee-awwww*!" he bellowed just as he did the day before. "*Hee-awwww*!"

That spunky red-spotted mule stopped in its tracks and didn't twitch a muscle. He stood there like a soldier at attention. Conan stared at him and snorted.

"Good mule, Conan," Colin said. "Good mule."

I looked behind the plow and saw a deep rut where it had dug into the field. "Colin, look what happened," I said. "We won't be able to plant anything there; it's too deep. Father will want us to fix it."

Colin agreed. "Let's fill it in and plow that part again. Help me, Finn."

I stood over the rut and looked at the torn soil. Something caught my attention. There was a small oval stone protruding from the soil. I picked it up and wiped it clean. A small, perfect hole pierced one of the ends. I couldn't imagine how it got there. The rest of the stone reminded me of a face. There were parts shaped like a mouth and eyes and a higher, flat spot that looked like a long nose.

"Colin, look what I found," I said to my brother, who was busy trying to control two mules. "What is it?" he asked.

"It's a stone," I said. "But I don't know what kind of a stone. It looks like a face."

"Let me see," Colin said. He took the stone in one hand and held the mule reins in the other.

"It's just a stone, Finn," he said. "The plow blade probably made those marks, that's all."

I wasn't sure I agreed with Colin's observation. My friends said the same thing whenever I thought I found arrowheads along the river. I always wound up leaving them there. This time I wasn't going to do that. I put the stone into my pocket and helped Colin with the mules.

That night in bed, I strung a leather lace through the hole in the stone and held my discovery up to the light of the lantern. I wondered what I had uncovered.

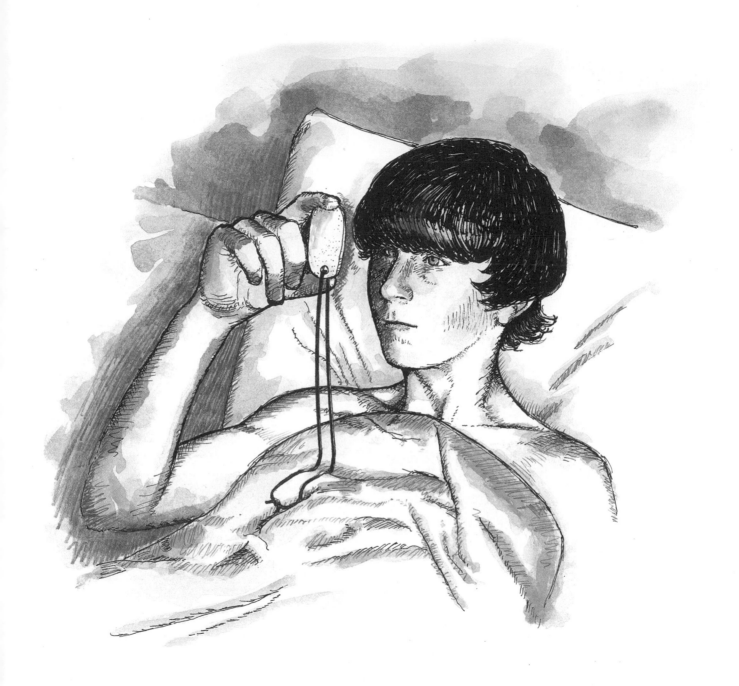

CHAPTER 8
CHARTING OUR COURSE

Father was extremely busy the final days before our trip. He worked long hours on the boat and also spent considerable time meeting people in Shimersville, Freemansburg, Bethlehem and Easton. Colin and I wondered why Father met these men. We received an explanation one night at supper.

"Boys, many boat captains don't own their own boat like I do," he told us. "They work for the company that built the canal, the Lehigh Coal and Navigation Company."

"Company boat captains get paid only for the time they work. When I bought the *Belfast Queen*, I knew that by being my own boss, no one would pay me for how long I work. I'll make money only if I make a profit on products I buy from suppliers and sell to customers. The men I've been meeting are business owners who make the products I plan to buy and deliver with the *Belfast Queen*."

I remember how confused I was when Father said that. Profit? I had never heard the word before. I felt just as I did when Mother taught me how to bake bread; I had no idea what she was talking about. With my kitchen lessons in mind, I spoke up.

"Father," I shyly said. "What is profit?"

"That's an important question, Finn," he said. "Maybe this will help. When we make our first trip on the Lehigh Canal, our destination is White Haven. It's a town about sixty miles north of here in the great Pocono Mountains.

"There are large lumber camps in the forests around White Haven. In the winter it gets very cold and the lumberjacks need warm clothing. I have made arrangements to deliver woolen cloth to White Haven. It will be made into coats, shirts, pants and scarves for the lumbermen.

"The cloth is made in Mr. Shimer's fulling mill along Saucon Creek. I have agreed to pay

him fifty cents for every yard of cloth
I buy. When we get to White Haven,
I will be paid one dollar for each yard.
The difference between what I am
paid for the cloth and what I pay
Mr. Shimer is the profit."

I understood that. I was pretty good
with numbers, so I did some quick figuring
in my head to determine Father's profit on each
yard of cloth.

"Father, you're going to get a profit of fifty cents on each yard," I proudly proclaimed. I remember
Colin looking at me like I was some kind of genius.

"Very good, Finn!" Father said. "You are right; the difference is fifty cents. But that is not my
profit because the Lehigh Coal and Navigation Company is going to charge me money for using its
canal. I have to pay them a toll of two cents for every mile we travel and also a portion of a penny
for every pound of cargo we carry on the *Belfast Queen*."

"That's not fair!" I said. "They're taking your profit."

"Son, that's part of the business," Father replied. "I must consider all of my costs before I can
count my profit. Everyone who owns a boat has to do the same thing."

From that moment on I understood that making money on the canal was not going to be easy.
I also understood that Father needed plenty of friendships in order to have enough products to buy
and sell. He started taking me to some of his meetings, thinking it would be good for me to know
what the *Belfast Queen* would be carrying.

I went with him to visit Mr. Knecht's iron foundry in Shimersville. I had no idea Mr. Knecht
made cast iron stoves and kettles and frying pans. They were just like those I used in mother's
kitchen. I also saw men making wagon parts and even flat irons for pressing clothes.

We also visited Mr. Dietz in Freemansburg. He was a tinsmith who came to America from
Germany. His shop was full of beautiful lamps and lanterns, coffee pots, canteens, cups, plates,
and lots of other things people along the canal needed.

Father's plan was to load the *Belfast Queen* with as many products as he could, and make a profit on all of them. He arranged to carry Mr. Geissinger's wheat flour; Mr. Reese's towline ropes; bricks made by Mr. Messinger, and salted meats cured in Mr. Fritchman's smokehouse.

One day Father put me on the back of Conan and we rode into Bethlehem. We stopped at a large lumber yard along the canal near Sand Island. It was owned by the same company that operated the lumber camps near White Haven.

Father went into an office and talked to a man for more than one hour. When he came outside he had a big smile on his face. He told me the man agreed to have Father supply six lumber camps near White Haven with new stoves, woolen cloth, and lots of rope, tin products, salted meat and wheat flour. The lumber company was buying far more than just the woolen cloth they agreed to buy a few weeks ago. To make the situation even better, Father was told he would be a regular carrier of the company's lumber on the return trips from White Haven. He was a happy man.

That night I heard Mother tell Father that she was worried he would not have enough money to buy everything he planned to take to White Haven. He tried very hard to put her mind at ease.

"Mary," he told her. "I have made good friends. They know how hard I work and how I saved to buy the *Belfast Queen*. They know we came here with nothing but a wagon and a mule.

"It's because I am honest and hard working that they are willing to do business with me. Each man is allowing me to pay for their goods when the trip is over. The lumber company will pay me when I arrive in White Haven. When I return to Freemansburg, I will use that money to pay my friends."

"Fergus," Mother told him. "I am proud of you. You have never strayed from your dream. The *Belfast Queen* will be a success with you as her captain."

MEETING NANCY

The *Belfast Queen* had been checked for leaks and was docked at one of Freemansburg's boat basins next to the canal. Father had painted the boat with a whitewash and now Colin and I were about to apply a second color. We were more than a little surprised when we found out what the color was.

"A boat named after a fine Irish city should be painted as green as the Emerald Isle itself," Father told us one morning at the basin. "Lads, here is the greenest paint I could find west of Belfast."

Green? Most boats were brown, and you could tell which were company boats because they had red-and-white bull's-eyes painted on the front and back. But green? No one had a green boat. Colin and I looked at each other and smiled. It was an unusual choice, but for Father, we would do our best to make the *Belfast Queen* look like a sparkling jewel.

Working at the boat basin allowed me to see how busy the canal was. Boats traveled in both directions, some going east toward Easton and others heading west to Bethlehem and Allentown and beyond. Mules shared the towpath without ever walking into each other.

Most of the boats were single boats with almost all of their interior space set aside for cargo. The Lehigh Coal and Navigation Company owned "hinge boats," which were two boats connected in the middle by large iron hinges and pins. The company boats always were loaded with coal, up to one hundred tons of it. Coal was the most important product carried on the canal. Workers at one of the coal yards told me it came from mines near White Haven and a town with the odd name of Mauch Chunk.

Coal was the fuel that was firing iron furnaces all over eastern Pennsylvania. People were even starting to use it to heat their homes. Coal was so valuable that it was called "black diamonds."

One afternoon while we were painting, Father called us together for a crew talk. We had a lot of them lately.

"Boys," he started, "what time have we been coming down here each morning to paint the boat?"

"Seven o'clock," Colin and I answered.

"Is the canal busy when we get here?"

"Yes, Father, it's very busy."

"Did you know it's busy because everyone is here three hours before we arrive?"

Three hours before we arrive, I thought. How could that be?

"Father," I said. "That would mean they start work at four o'clock in the morning. No one works that early…do they?"

"No," Father said, "they don't. They start even earlier, at three o'clock when they get out of bed to groom the mules, prepare the boat and eat breakfast."

I didn't know whose mouth dropped open wider, Colin's or mine.

Then came more surprising news.

"We will be traveling on the canal six days a week, from four o'clock in the morning to ten o'clock at night. That's when the canal is open for business, and that's when we will be on it. We won't be working on Sundays; it's a day of rest and the canal is closed."

If Colin had been wearing shoes, I think he would have jumped right out of them.

"Father, that means we get only five hours of sleep each night," he said. "I don't know if I can do that."

I hoped Colin's mild protest would change Father's mind, but it didn't.

"I know this will be hard, but all of us will get used to it," Father said. "There are hundreds of other boat families who do this. We can do it, too.

"We start our new sleep schedule tonight. Tomorrow morning we'll wake up at three o'clock and practice our jobs at the boat. Colin, you'll bring Conan and Rogan along. We leave on our trip on Monday, so we don't have much time to learn."

We were shocked. Father looked at our sullen faces. I knew he felt bad. He told us to clean our paint brushes and spend the rest of the afternoon with our friends, but I was not in the mood for a good time.

I walked toward Main Street and turned north. I came to Geissinger's Grist Mill. Jennie was helping her mother wash clothes and she waved to me. Normally that would have brought a big smile to my face, but I didn't even wave back.

A little stream called Nancy Run flowed by Mr. Geissinger's mill. I decided to follow it and look for arrowheads. Whenever I looked for Indian things, I'd take my stone out from underneath my shirt and let it dangle in the open. I didn't tell anybody why I did that, but secretly it made me feel a little like an Indian.

My stone wasn't shiny, but that day it seemed to reflect every ray of the sun that was coming through the trees. The reflections bounced back into the sky, onto the ground and even down to the water. I was beginning to forget my new sleep schedule when one of the reflections landed on a small, three-sided rock with thin, sharp edges.

"I found one!" I shouted. "Good gracious, this time I have found one for sure."

I was so happy that I was unaware I was not alone.

"Boy, what are you doing here?" said a voice from above the stream. "What do you have there?"

I was caught by surprise. I was sure I had been alone. My eyes looked up to the top of the stream bank. Standing there was an old woman wearing a long dress, a long-sleeved blouse, a woolen shawl and a bonnet tied under her chin. Her hair was gray and her hands and face were very dark brown, almost black. I had never seen a person with that color skin.

"Boy! Are you deaf?" she said. "I asked you what you found."

I stammered. I was still surprised. Where had she come from?

"Why…ma'am," I slowly started. "I think I've found an arrowhead."

"I know that's an arrowhead," she told me. "I'm asking you about that stone you have hung around your neck. Let me see it."

I stepped out of the creek and walked up next to her. I wasn't afraid of this woman. She sounded gruff, but she had a wise smile in her eyes. Her hand reached out and she cupped the stone in her palm. She stared intently at it and then asked me a question.

"Boy, did you find this?"

"Yes, ma'am, I did," I replied. "I found it in the cornfield behind our house, up on the hill above Shimersville."

Her eyes widened and a smile broke over her face.

"On the hill above Shimersville," she repeated. "I'll bet you found arrowheads over there, too."

"Well, ma'am, I thought I did but my friends told me they were just sharp rocks."

"Your friends don't know what they're talking about," the woman said. "Shimersville is home to a lot of Indian things from the past. People just don't know where to look for them. You found something I haven't seen in a long time."

"What is it?" I asked.

The old woman looked at me and then turned her eyes toward the tree tops. She stared and looked like she was praying, only her eyes were wide open. Her hand clenched the stone. I watched and hoped she'd say something.

"Keep your stone with you, boy," she finally said in a quiet voice. "Keep it with you all your days. It will help you understand the way of the world."

"Help me understand the world? But how?" I asked.

"In time, boy," she answered. "You will learn in time."

And then she began to walk away. I called out to her and asked her name. She turned around and smiled.

"My name is Nancy," she said. "They named this little stream Nancy Run after me. Come back and visit me again."

CHAPTER 10

A MORNING TO REMEMBER

Monday, the 24th of September, 1855, began with three words I will never forget. "Finn, wake up!"

It was Father, captain of the *Belfast Queen*, ordering his cook out of bed and down to the boat basin in Freemansburg. This was not practice; it was the first day of our long-awaited trip on the Lehigh Canal. But why did it have to start at three o'clock in the morning? My eyelids had a difficult time opening.

Colin was already harnessing Conan and Rogan. Father was loading the last of the food supplies onto our wagon. Mother was up, too, and was dressing little Rose for the ride across the river to Freemansburg. This was one event she did not want to miss.

The five of us boarded the wagon and rode in darkness to the covered bridge. As we approached we could see lanterns across the river in Freemansburg. We were not the only people awake.

The *Belfast Queen* was docked at the boat basin owned by Mr. Lerch and Mr. Knauss next to Washington Street. When we arrived, Colin unhitched the mules and walked them toward the towpath. I carried the food supplies into the boat's crew cabin. Mother and Rose followed me.

The cabin was only about eight feet long and ten feet wide. A man six feet tall might bump his head on the ceiling. Our straw beds and a little dinner table were folded up against the wall to save room.

My job was to get the cooking stove lighted and breakfast started. I had to be really careful. An accident could burn the *Belfast Queen* and everything it carried. I started the fire with wood and added chunks of coal as the embers got hotter. Coal fires got a lot hotter and lasted a lot longer than wood.

Freemansburg was wide awake even though there wasn't an ounce of daylight in the sky. Mule drivers were brushing their mules and making sure feed bags were full. Captains were preparing to throw towlines from the boats to the towpath. They shouted instructions to their crews.

There were wives and small children on some of the boats. Some of the women were cooking and others were lighting big "nighthawker" oil lamps that hung from posts in the front of the boats. They had shiny reflectors attached to them that cast light onto the canal and towpath. It was a good way for boats to see each other in the darkness. I took a good sniff of the air. My nostrils filled with the heavenly scent of fried bacon.

"Finn, how is breakfast coming along?" Father called from the deck.

"Just fine, Father," I answered. "It will be ready soon."

Of course Father didn't know that Mother had secretly given me a head start. She had taken little Rose into the cabin and was nearly finished preparing a fine meal of flapjacks, eggs and smokehouse bacon.

"Mary, we're about to go," Father shouted. "Where are you?"

"I'm down here, Fergus, with Rose and Finn," Mother answered from the cabin. "Your breakfast is ready. We'll bring the food to the deck." I heard Father chuckle.

Colin tied the mules to Father's wagon and joined us. Mother and little Rose sat on the mules' feed box while the Captain and his crew found space on the long bin that held the stove's coal supply.

In the distance we heard odd noises that sounded like sad cows letting out long, melancholy moos. There was one after another.

"What are those noises, Father?" I asked.

"Those are the boats saying, 'Good morning!' to each other, Finn," he replied. "Colin, show your brother how we say that."

Colin reached into the feed box and pulled out an odd-looking object. I didn't know what it was, but Colin did. He held one end of it to his mouth, took a deep breath and blew into it as hard as he could.

"OW-OOOOOOOO! OW-OOOOOOOO!"

Little Rose buried her head under Mother's coat and started crying. I looked at my brother's very proud face and started laughing.

"Good gracious, what is that thing?" I asked. "Where did it come from?"

"It's a conch shell," Colin said. "It's a horn to signal locktenders and other people, to let them

know we're coming down the canal. Father got it from Mr. Knauss. He said it comes from the ocean. I'll teach you how to use it."

"Boys, it's almost four o'clock," Father said, patting each of us on our shoulders. "Our first day of business on the canal is about to begin. Let's say good-bye to Mother and Rose."

I saw tears trickle down Mother's cheeks. Father told her we would be back in one week, but nothing was ever definite on the canal. It was not easy for her, or us, to part ways.

"Mary, the boys and I will take care of each other," Father said. "We will be safe. Mr. Knecht will be here soon with one of his horses. He'll hitch it to the wagon and take you and Rose home. He'll check in on you every day while we're gone. Everything will be fine."

We all hugged Mother. Colin helped her and little Rose off the boat and then walked to Conan and Rogan. The towline from the boat was attached to their harness and the mules headed down the towpath with Colin behind them. The slack towline rope tightened and rose from the water as they walked further down the path. The *Belfast Queen* started moving very slowly. Father held the steering rudder with one hand and waved to Mother with the other. I waved, too, and watched as she and Rose became smaller and smaller.

"We're on our way, Father." I said, straining to see down the canal. "We're really on our way."

I looked to the east and saw the faint light of early morning. I could detect movement all around me. Conch shells blared ahead of us. I looked up at Father and saw the confident smile of a proud man whose dream had finally come true.

CHAPTER 11
White Haven or Bust!

I was a little nervous as Father steered the *Belfast Queen* through the canal. I had painted the boat, loaded it and cooked on it, but I was never on it when it moved. I clutched my Indian stone through my shirt. It seemed to comfort me.

The sky was becoming brighter. I looked toward the towpath and there was Colin, leading Conan and Rogan like they were two huge pets.

"Colin, I see you!" I called to him. "It's working!"

He waved quickly. I could tell he was very focused on his job. There was a boat in front of us and one behind. Colin had to make sure the mules moved at a pace that wouldn't cause collisions.

"Are the dishes clean, Finn?" Father asked.

Oops. I was so involved in what was going on around me that I forgot I was a member of a crew.

"I'll get to them right now, Father," I said, and down the ladder and into the cabin I went.

We were gone less than ten minutes before we began to slow down. I heard the sound of conch shells and climbed to the deck to see what was happening.

"Whoa, mules!" I heard Colin tell Conan and Rogan. "Whoa!"

"What's the problem, Father?" I asked.

"No problem, Finn," he replied. "We're coming to a lock. We're stopping to wait until it's our turn to go through."

I looked ahead of us. In the brightening light I saw a line of boats against the canal bank. Father steered us in and we came to a gentle stop behind the last one. Colin and the mules waited, just like every other driver and team I could see. I threw Colin a flapjack and Father handed him the feed bags, which he clipped to the mules' bridles.

A man whom Father called the "bank boss" walked along the towpath and made sure everything was going smoothly.

"Mr. Meyer, are the boats coming through

on time?" I heard him shout to a man walking near a little house next to the lock.

"Yes, sir, Mr. Johnson, they are," came a reply. "We're passing them at just under five minutes."

Father sat down with me next to our barrel of drinking water and explained what was going on.

"Finn, the canal is built along the river through miles and miles of hills and valleys," he said. "Just look to your right and you'll see the hills that lead to White Haven. In order for boats to get up and down those hills, the owners of the canal designed steps than can lift the boats or lower them, depending on which direction they're going. The steps are called locks."

"What lifts the boats once they are inside the locks, Father?" I asked. "Mules?"

"No," he said. "Water lifts the boats. In about ten minutes you're going to see how."

I watched the canal. Two boats floated past us headed toward Freemansburg. Then two in our line moved closer to the lock. I could tell the boats were taking turns doing something.

Suddenly the bank boss shouted to Father.

"*Belfast Queen*, are you ready to enter Lock 43?"

"Yes, Mr. Johnson, we are!" Father responded.

"Colin, take the mules down the path," Father shouted. "Finn, coil the short ropes."

Our boat eased toward the little house. The man named Mr. Meyer and two boys were busy turning iron wheels that were underneath little red shacks on both sides of the lock. I heard one of the boys call the shacks "dog houses."

The lock was made of two long, parallel walls of stone blocks. Each wall, as well as the floor of the lock, was covered with tightly-fitted wooden planks that protected the boats from the rough stone. The canal water flowed between the walls. I estimated each wall was about ten feet high and far enough apart so two boats could squeeze in side-by-side.

"Colin, here, catch the towline," Father yelled as he threw the heavy rope to the bank. "Finn, throw that lad one of the short ropes. He'll be able to pull us into the lock."

"Who is that boy?" I asked Father.

"It's one of Mr. Meyer's sons," Father replied. "Mr. Meyer is the locktender and that's the lock-tender's house where he and his family live. Throw the rope, son. He's waiting."

I was learning that life on the canal was lickety-split. Everybody moved fast and no one wasted time. I made a perfect throw to Mr. Meyer's son.

"What's your name?" I shouted. "I'm Finn Gorman."

"I'm Joseph Meyer," came the reply.

"Pleased to meet you, Joe," I told him. "I hope to see you on the way back."

The bank boss directed the boat in front of us to enter the lock and swing to the other side of the canal. Another boy caught a rope from the captain and slowly pulled the boat against the lock wall. Joe Meyer took our rope and pulled us in. We settled alongside the first boat, just an inch away. Ahead of us was a huge wooden drop gate that kept the canal water from entering the lock. As I looked up, I was a little scared that the drop gate would fail and the whole Lehigh Canal would rush in on top of us.

All of a sudden two gates behind us started to close.

"Father, what's happening?" I said as I clutched a boat post next to me. "I don't like this."

"We're okay," he assured me. "Watch."

The swing gates behind us closed tightly together, and water started rushing in from the bottom of the lock. We floated straight up like a cork and rose higher as more water entered from below. I looked at the little children on the boat next to us and they were laughing out loud. I felt a little foolish being so scared.

In less than five minutes, the water level inside the lock was equal with the water level on the other side of the drop gate. In fact, the drop gate wasn't there anymore. Some part of the process caused it to lower itself. All I could see in front of us was an open canal with lots of moving boats. I shook my head in disbelief at how well the lock worked.

Colin threw the towline back to Father and within seconds Conan and Rogan were pulling us up the towpath. I stood and watched everything around me.

"Father, we did it!" I shouted.

"Yes, Finn, we did. Are those dishes cleaned yet?"

"Right away, Captain," I said. "And your coffee will be on deck in a minute."

The *Belfast Queen* passed through thirteen more locks that day and made its way past Bethlehem, Allentown, Catasauqua, Stemton, Newport, Siegfried's Bridge, and Treichler's Station. That night we moored at a boat basin south of a little canal village called Lockport. Colin took the mules to a nearby barn and when he returned, I served a meal of ham, potatoes, carrots and my first loaf of baked bread. We were quite exhausted, and had no problem resting in the cabin.

"We have done well, boys," Father said. "I am very pleased. Let us give thanks for a fine start and a wonderful meal."

After supper we went on deck and gazed at the stars. One shot across the sky and disappeared in the north.

"That's our lucky star," Father said. "It's leading us to White Haven."

We all smiled. An owl hooted in a nearby pine tree and my eyes began to droop. The lantern light in the cabin drew us to our straw beds and we stretched out and closed our eyes for the night. I clutched my stone and drifted into a deep sleep.

CHAPTER 12
INTO THE MOUNTAINS

Waking up on Tuesday wasn't any easier than Monday, but it was gentler. "Good morning, Finn," Father said as he tapped my shoulder and lighted the cabin lantern. "Colin, good morning. How are your feet this morning?"

"They're okay, Father. A little stiff, that's all."

"Maybe today you'll wear the shoes I bought you," Father added on his way up the cabin ladder. "Your feet may thank you."

My brother did not wear shoes in spring, summer or fall unless he was in church or school. I was hoping Monday's twenty-two-mile walk on the towpath had changed his way of thinking.

"Father got you nice sturdy shoes, Colin. Why don't you wear them?"

"I'll see what happens today," he said. "I have to get Conan and Rogan. Will you throw some flapjacks to me when they're ready?"

Lockport was every bit as busy as Freemansburg. There were nighthawkers lighted everywhere. A lot of boats must have come in after us. I brewed Father's coffee and took it to him.

"Where are we headed today, Father?"

"Mauch Chunk," he said. "It's a coal town along the Lehigh about twenty miles from here. That's not too far, but we have to go through twenty-seven locks to get there. It will be a long day."

The sound of conch shells filled the air a few minutes before four o'clock. The canal was opening for business and the *Belfast Queen* was entering its second day in operation.

As darkness turned to daylight, we came to a spot where the canal had to cross a stream. Someone was smart enough to design a bridge that carried the canal. It had the shape of a huge trough and was supported by several large stone pillars. Father called it an aqueduct. While we floated through it, Colin and the mules walked across on a narrow wooden walkway. I was hoping Colin didn't pick up any splinters in his bare feet.

The scenery became prettier as we headed north. It was late in the growing season and crops were in full harvest. I could see farmers in the nearby fields cutting hay and corn with long scythes. Most settlements we passed had mills where corn and wheat were ground into flour. I used both types of flour to make my flapjacks and bread.

We passed through three locks before we reached Walnutport. Everybody called it "locking through," so we started saying it, too. As we proceeded, we got closer and closer to a huge mountain I had been watching for miles. It must have been a thousand feet tall and it stretched out on both sides of the river as far as I could see.

"That's Blue Mountain," Father said. "And that little settlement at the bottom is Lehigh Water Gap. It was named after the river and the opening in the mountain. People say that Blue Mountain stretches all the way down to Maryland and all the way up to New York."

I gazed upward and saw groups of large birds soaring above everything. Their outstretched wings did not move. They simply let the wind carry them across the river and out of sight. Father saw me watching them and looked up as well.

"They're eagles, Father," I said, not knowing how I knew. "They're on a journey to their winter home. They make the same journey every year."

Father looked at me with a raised eyebrow. "How do you know that, son?" he asked. "Have you ever seen an eagle?"

"No, I haven't," I said. "I know it sounds strange, but I felt like I heard them telling me their story."

Father looked at me and scratched his head, but then turned his attention to Colin and the mules. "There's another aqueduct ahead," he said. "Stay alert."

We passed over the aqueduct at Lehigh Gap and locked through eleven more locks before arriving in Weissport, where Father decided to tie up for supper.

"It's only four o'clock, but we'll stop and eat," he said. "We must get to Mauch Chunk by ten o'clock. We have six more miles and eight more locks. Colin, how are your feet?"

"They're fine, Father, better than yesterday," he said.

Father laughed and looked at me.

"He is stubborn, isn't he?" he whispered.

"Father, I think he's trying to show you he's not afraid to do hard work," I quietly replied.

"Maybe," Father said. "But there's nothing wrong with doing hard work in a pair of shoes. We need his feet. It's a long trip."

Colin tied the mules and filled their feed bags with oats. Father gathered a small sack of coal and walked toward Lock 8. He came back with a sack full of fresh tomatoes and squash and a leafy head of lettuce.

"Locktender families are good gardeners," Father said as he handed me the vegetables. "Winter is coming and they need coal, so I bartered them a sack of coal for a sack of fresh vegetables. I also paid five cents for a chicken. Remember about bartering, Finn. It's going to be your chore from now on."

I cooked a fine dinner that evening in Weissport. After we finished, Colin went for Conan and Rogan and I cleaned the dishes. A family on another boat was singing a song I'd heard often since we left Freemansburg. I liked it. I didn't know all the words, but the end of each verse was easy to remember.

> *Oh! Susanna, don't you cry for me;*
> *I come from Alabama,*
> *with my banjo on my knee*

I thought I'd try to learn more of the words as we continued our trip.

Colin was gone longer than Father liked. When he got back, I couldn't believe my eyes. He was holding two big floppy straw hats and two cow bells that jingled every time he took a step. I didn't know what to say, but Father did.

"Colin, how did you get those?" he asked in a stern voice I hadn't heard too often. "Who are they for?"

"They're for Conan and Rogan, Father," he said sheepishly. "All the mules wear them. Hats keep the sun out of their eyes and the bugs off their heads. The bells will let us know where they are all the time."

I liked the hats and bells, but considering the look on Father's face, I wasn't about to say so.

"How did you get them, Colin? You don't have any money."

"I bartered for them, Father," Colin replied. "Just like you did for the vegetables. I bartered my shoes for the hats and bells."

I prayed for my brother at that moment. After hearing from Father how much we needed Colin's feet, I didn't know how he was going to react. Once you make a barter, the barter is done and can't be reversed. Colin was stuck without a pair of shoes.

"Colin," Father began. "I bought those shoes for this trip and other trips ahead. But if you chose to barter them, that is your decision and you will have to live without shoes.

"I like the hats and bells, Colin, but if you need shoes, you will buy them yourself. We have three good shoemakers in Freemansburg."

Father always had a way of making his point without yelling. I breathed a sigh of relief, and Colin ran to give the mules their gifts. Conan tried to chew his hat and Rogan spooked when he heard the bell. But soon they were adorned with the finest mule attire north of Freemansburg. The towline was attached to the *Belfast Queen* and we set course for Mauch Chunk.

The land around us changed quickly. Small hills became taller and rose steeply from each side of the river. The locks became longer and higher and appeared more frequently. I felt we must be entering the great Pocono Mountains Father told us about. Finally, we arrived at Mauch Chunk. Lock 1 below the town was busy and it took us until nearly ten o'clock to lock through and find a mooring spot for the night. Hundreds of lights twinkled across the river.

"Colin, tie the mules and come into the cabin," Father said. "We have another long day tomorrow."

CHAPTER **13**

LIONS AND BEARS

Our morning in Mauch Chunk was brief. Father woke us at three o'clock sharp and had us ready to move in less than one hour. I strained my eyes, but it was too dark to see what was happening across the river.

"We'll be back here in two days, Finn," Father said. "You'll have plenty of time then to see it in daylight. There are twenty-nine locks and twenty dams between us and White Haven. We must be on our way. We have to reach White Haven by evening."

As the sky brightened, I could see that the hills we passed in Weissport had turned to mountains on both sides of the river. We were traveling through a steep gorge that went on and on and on. The air was chilly enough to cause my breath to turn to vapor. I looked at Colin's bare feet and shook my head.

We traveled past four dams and seven locks by eight o'clock. We also crossed the river at two places where the mountain was so steep on one side that there was no room for a towpath. Colin and the mules crossed on bridges. The

Belfast Queen was attached to a thick wire cable and pulled across.

There were dams and locks everywhere. The dams were tall and made of gigantic logs and rocks. They backed up pools of water as big as lakes. Wherever there was a pool, there was no canal. The mules simply walked on a towpath that followed the river bank, just like at Lehigh Gap. Because there were so many dams and pools, the mules followed the river bank most of the day. Father heard a man say there were only five miles of real canal between Mauch Chunk and White Haven. I told him that meant twenty-one miles of the towpath were on the river bank. I was always good with numbers.

The locks got taller and longer as we went north. A lot of them were built at one end of a dam, with only a very short section of canal leading in or out. There were many times when we reached the end of one pool and stared up at another dam and lock. Once we locked through, we were immediately in the next pool.

Despite their enormous size, it never took us more than three minutes to lock through any of them, even Lock 27, which lifted us thirty feet. We heard from other people that the rocks of the lock walls were cut so precisely that they were able to be pieced together without cement. I wondered how many men and mules it took to build them.

Even though I had never been in these mountains, I felt oddly at home. I saw animals throughout the day, although whenever I called to Father to share my discoveries, they were gone. One time I looked up and saw a tan-colored cat so big that it looked like an African lion without long hair on its head.

Another time I saw a bear walking along a trail cut high into the mountain slope. It stopped and gave me a long stare. Suddenly I heard a loud crack and saw the bear tumble down the hill to the edge of the river. A man on the boat behind us laughed loudly and then shouted to his mule driver.

"I got it, Jacob!" he yelled. "I got that bear square on. We'll have meat for the next two weeks. Tie the mules and go get it."

My chest burned like I was being stuck with a hot poker. It was my Indian stone. It was as hot as a piece of coal. I pulled the leather string off my neck and looked back at the man holding the rifle.

"Mister, you had no right to shoot that bear!" I shouted. I was more furious than I had ever been in my life. Colin stopped the mules and Father turned around and told me to mind my mouth.

"That bear belonged to the forest, Father," I said. "That man gave no warning to the bear. He just shot it and laughed. He had no respect."

Father tried to calm me down. The stone was cooling and I began to gain my composure. But I was still mad, and not ready to be quiet.

"Mister, that bear won't be fit for eating," I yelled back to the boat behind us. "You and your crew will get sick if you eat it."

"Finn, that's enough!" Father ordered. "I won't have you talking like that to another boat captain, no matter what he did. Now let's get on our way. Colin, get Conan and Rogan back on the towpath. We need to be in White Haven before dark."

I didn't say another word, nor did I look at the boat behind us the rest of the way. I took a close look at my stone. The lines that Colin thought were cut by the plow blade looked more and more like eyes and a mouth. I was sure the high, flat part between them was a nose. I remembered how the old woman Nancy stared at it that day along the stream in Freemansburg.

"Get ready to lock through," Father shouted as we approached Lock 28. I looked ahead and saw another enormous lock. Within minutes, we were thirty feet higher and in another long pool.

"One more to go, boys, and we'll be in White Haven," Father said. "Finn, are you alright?"

"Yes, Father, I feel better," I responded, although the bear was still on my mind.

Lock 29 came up quickly. We locked through and traveled a short distance along the bank of the great pool behind Dam 20. Then we entered a small lock and were lowered into a short canal that led into White Haven.

"Boys, we made it," Father said. "And we made it on time. I'm very proud of you. Tomorrow the men from the lumber camp will meet us to unload the boat. Tonight we'll take Conan and Rogan to a mule stable and have dinner at a hotel."

I wasn't in the best of moods that night. It had been an exciting yet frustrating day. I sat in the White Haven Hotel thinking about the bear and the old woman Nancy and what she had said about my stone.

It will help you understand the way of the world, my mind kept repeating.

Whose world? I wondered. It was still a mystery to me.

CHAPTER 14
CHIP OFF THE OLD BLOCK

I opened my eyes to something very different the next morning: daylight. Father let us sleep in. I heard him on the deck opening cargo hatches so the boat could be unloaded. Then his footsteps came toward the cabin.

"Finn, are you awake?" he whispered down the cabin hatch. I laughed to myself. Father had the ears of a dog.

"Yes, sir," I said. "What time is it?"

"Almost six o'clock. Please wake your brother and ask him to come on deck. Can you cook one of your delicious breakfasts?"

"Yes, Father," I told him. "But I don't have any eggs. Will ham and sliced potatoes be alright?"

"That sounds good to me, Finn," Father replied. "I'll give you money to buy fresh eggs in White Haven."

I prepared breakfast and received the rest of my daily orders. Colin and Father were going to help unload the *Belfast Queen*. I was to buy eggs and have plenty of coffee ready on the cabin stove. Other than that, all I had to do was help load the lighter cargo onto the wagons.

"Here's fifty cents for the eggs," Father said. I walked off the boat and started searching for a grocery store. Everywhere I looked I saw something that was related to lumber. There were canal boats loaded with freshly cut wooden planks. I saw sawmills along the river with huge piles of logs stacked behind them. Everywhere I walked I heard the high-pitched sound of saw wheels cutting through fresh wood. White Haven was certainly a lumber town.

Finally I saw a grocery store on the corner of Hemlock Street and Railroad Street.

Railroad Street? I thought to myself. *There's a railroad here?*

Railroads were new. During the summer I watched one being built on the Shimersville side of the Lehigh River. It required a lot of people to lay down the crushed rock bed and build the tracks. A month before we left on our trip, a big steam engine roared down the track from Bethlehem and passed Shimersville. It pulled a car full of people and a few cars loaded with coal. The engine had lettering on it that read *Lehigh Valley Railroad*. The people waved to us as they went by. Father didn't like it. He said that one day the railroad would put canal boats out of business.

White Haven's railroad was different. There weren't any tracks going through town. All I could find was a building with a sign that read *Lehigh and Susquehanna Railroad* and a big loading area next to it. The only tracks I saw went out of White Haven and over the mountains to the north.

I asked a man about this railroad. He told me it was built to bring coal to White Haven from mines near Wilkes-Barre. He said the men who owned the railroad also owned the mines and the canal.

I walked into *Myers Dry Goods and Grocery Store* and told the man behind the counter I needed as many eggs as I could get for two silver quarters. He carefully put four dozen of them in a cloth sack and gave me two copper pennies as change. I put them into my pocket and headed back to the boat basin.

When I arrived, four long wagons were pulled up next to the *Belfast Queen* and everyone was busy unloading something. The first thing I noticed about the men from the lumber camps was that they all had beards.

"Watch those stoves," one of them shouted. "We need them for the new camp."

I gave Father the two pennies and went down to the cabin to put the eggs in the food locker. When I went back on deck, I noticed a boy sitting on one of the wagons. He looked bored. I jumped off the boat and went over to say hello.

"Can I sit in your wagon?" I asked. "My name is Finn Gorman."

"Sure, come on up," he said. "I'm Robert Kern, but you can call me Chip."

"Chip? That's a lot different than Robert."

"It's my nickname," he said. "The men at the camp say my Pa and I look and act so much alike, that I'm just like a 'chip off the old block.' So, they call me Chip."

"Which one of those men is your Pa?" I asked.

"The one with the red shirt and suspenders," Chip replied.

"Well," I said, "if you're a chip off the old block, where's your beard?"

We both giggled. I told Chip what we were doing in White Haven and he told me about living at a lumber camp.

"You live at a lumber camp?" I asked, thinking lumber camps were only for grown men.

"Sure, my Ma and sister are there, too," Chip said. "Ma cooks at the mess hall and Emma helps. I help, too. I cut carrots and potatoes and make sure the kitchen is clean. Ma also lets me bake pies." It was nice to know Chip and I had something in common.

"Do you think you can take me to see the lumber camp?" I asked my new friend.

"Well, I'll ask Pa," Chip said. "Maybe you can go with us when we take the wagons back. You could eat supper with us, too, and Pa could bring you back. Of course your Pa will have to say it's alright."

"Father!" I yelled from the wagon. "Can I go with Chip to the lumber camp?"

After explaining our plan, Father and Mr. Kern agreed to let me go. I had to be back by sunset. When the boat was unloaded, Mr. Kern directed Father to the lumber company's office where Father would receive payment for the goods he brought from Freemansburg.

"Take care of my son," he told Mr. Kern. "And thank you for allowing him to see your camp." Mr. Kern snapped the horse's reins and off we went.

CHAPTER 15

LUMBERJACKS AND APPLE PIE

Two large horses pulled each of the lumber camp wagons. Mr. Kern took the lead wagon and headed out of White Haven on a narrow dirt road. Chip and I sat on the seat next to him. I paid close attention to everything I saw.

I found it confusing that the land outside White Haven had so few trees. If we were going to a lumber camp, where was the forest? All I saw were huge stumps in the ground and lots of small bushes. If there were trees, they weren't near White Haven. We drove west for nearly an hour before I finally began to see green in the distance.

"Is that where your camp is, Mr. Kern?" I asked.

"Close to there, boy," he replied. "Once we get to those trees, we have to ride another thirty minutes to reach the camp. We built it pretty far into the forest."

The bumpy ride continued. The trees I saw from a distance now loomed right in front of me. They were absolutely huge. I'd never seen anything like them.

"Chip, what kind of trees are they?" I asked my new friend.

"White pines and hemlocks," Chip said. "They're hundreds of years old and each one has enough wood in it to build a house or two."

The road became shadier as we entered the forest. At some places it was almost dark. I had an odd feeling that I was in the company of old friends. I stared up at the pines and hemlocks and felt like their branches were huge arms reaching out to give me shelter and protection.

We drove a little further and I began hearing the sound of saws and hammers. We turned a corner in the road and entered a clearing where there were large white tents and brand new log buildings, some of them still not complete. There were men on the ground sawing boards and others on the buildings hammering the boards into place.

"This is our new camp," Mr. Kern said. "The mess hall is built. That's where we cook and eat. This new building is going to be the bunkhouse, where the men will sleep. Right now they're sleeping in those tents, but we want to have the bunkhouse built before winter sets in."

The buildings were larger than any in Freemansburg, especially the bunkhouse. "How many men work here?" I asked Chip.

"About one hundred," he said. "But I've visited some camps that have more than two hundred men."

"I guess people need a lot of wood," I said.

"Finn, we can sell all the trees we cut," Mr. Kern said. "America is growing, and it needs lumber, a lot of it. This is just one of hundreds of camps along the Lehigh and Delaware rivers. The lumberjacks in those camps cut hundreds of thousands of pines and hemlocks each year. That wood is building towns and cities and industries from White Haven to Philadelphia. It's building canal boats and ships and supplying lumber for bridges and railroads and even wagons for the Army.

"Once we unload these wagons, Chip and I will take you where the trees are being cut. Please come in and meet my wife and daughter."

Mrs. Kern was a tall woman with rosy cheeks and a cheerful smile. She and Emma were in the mess hall rolling enough dough to make crust for twenty-five apple pies. There were sacks of flour stacked in a corner of the kitchen and pie tins everywhere. Next to Emma was a large tin canister filled with lard. Now I knew why Father brought so much flour and tin goods from Freemansburg.

"Welcome, Finn, it's nice to meet you," Mrs. Kern said. "I'm happy you can join us. Do you know how to peel apples?"

Mrs. Kern didn't know she was talking to another baker.

"Yes, Mrs. Kern, I can help," I replied. "May I have a paring knife?"

Chip chuckled. "A paring knife won't do much good here, Finn," he said. "We have too many apples to peel. We have something better."

He reached under a large wooden table and pulled out a cast iron device that had geared wheels and a crank handle. There was a sharp blade on one side and a clamp on the bottom.

"It's an apple parer, Finn," Chip said. "Didn't you ever see one? You just clamp it to the table, stick an apple on that big thick needle and adjust the blade so it touches the apple. When you turn the handle, the apple turns and the blade cuts off the skin. I can do one in about ten seconds."

Peeling apples was never so much fun. Chip and I were done in no time. Emma took out the cores, cut the apples into pieces and placed them in the pie tins that Mrs. Kern had just lined with freshly rolled dough.

"Lumberjacks must like apple pies," I said.

"Lumberjacks like everything," Mrs. Kern laughed. "We work all day just to prepare breakfast and supper for them. They eat more food than anyone I know."

Our job was done in the kitchen. Mr. Kern was waiting outside with a smaller wagon and a fresh horse. We drove deeper into the forest. The pines and hemlocks were so thick that they blocked the sun from reaching the forest floor. Nothing grew underneath them.

Then I heard a sound I'd never heard before, a low, rumbling noise that lasted a couple of seconds and shook the ground. I thought a fairy tale giant was walking toward us.

"What was that?" I said, hoping for an answer that didn't have anything to do with giants.

"It was a tree falling," Chip said. "Probably a hemlock. They're a little bigger and heavier than pines and make louder noises when they fall."

Then I heard another, and another. As we drove farther down the winding road, the noises became louder and the ground shook even more. Suddenly Mr. Kern pulled back the reins of his horse.

"TIMBERRRR!" came a loud shout from the forest. And with that, I heard a crashing sound so close that I felt whatever it was, it was going to crash right on top of me. I jumped out of the wagon just as the ground shook and was knocked off my feet. I was scared. But when I looked at Chip, he was trying his best not to laugh.

"Are you alright, Finn?" Mr. Kern asked. "Don't worry; we're not close enough to get hurt."

I didn't answer Mr. Kern. I felt the oddest sensation come over me. I heard high-pitched sounds and then looked at the fallen tree. Its stump was oozing lots of sap and its branches were slowly folding toward its trunk.

"That tree was a grandfather of this forest, and so were the others I heard falling as we rode in," I said. "I know we need their wood but they were also needed by the animals of the forest. Didn't you hear the birds cry when the tree fell?"

Mr. Kern gave me a bewildered look and didn't quite know what to say.

"Finn, I never thought of it like that," he finally answered, looking at the fallen hemlock.

"I understand what you're saying, but we have a job to do and our job is to cut trees."

"Yes, Mr. Kern, I understand, too," I replied. "I'm sorry I got angry. Can we ride back to camp now?"

My stone was warm against my chest on the ride back to camp. I looked at the land around me and began to see it as it was before the lumberjacks arrived. I imagined deer and elk and bears and wolves and the singing of a multitude of birds. It was a magical place where time was measured not in days but in centuries.

But now there was nothing but miles of stumps and deep ruts gouged into the soil by rushing rainwater. When the forest grandfathers were cut, the rest of the life in the forest disappeared with them.

Supper at the lumber camp was at five o'clock. I had never sat down to supper with one hundred men before, but it was fun watching them talk and laugh and eat. One of them said he grew up in Freemansburg.

I enjoyed the meal Mrs. Kern and Emma made and thanked them for their hospitality. Mrs. Kern told me to thank Father for bringing the stoves and tinware and all the other supplies.

My Indian stone had cooled down when we arrived at the camp for supper, but now as we were back on the lifeless dirt road to White Haven, it was warming up again. I kept hearing the voice of the old woman Nancy over and over in my mind.

It will help you understand the way of the world.

I was beginning to understand what she meant, although I was not sure I liked it. That night I slept in the *Belfast Queen* holding my Indian stone, hoping it would help me understand more.

CHAPTER 16
BACK TO MAUCH CHUNK

As Father had told us over and over, his goal as a boat captain was to make a profit. That meant the *Belfast Queen* could not travel from town to town without carrying something that would put money in Father's pocket.

Just after sunrise, five long wagons from one of White Haven's sawmills pulled up in front of the boat basin. Each was loaded with short, thick timbers that would be taken to Mauch Chunk on the *Belfast Queen*. I watched as the sawmill workers carried them onto our boat.

"They're called railroad ties," Father said as he watched the men stack the timbers in the boat's cargo space. "I'm not anxious to supply something for a railroad, but I'm being paid a good price to deliver them, so I will."

We were well rested and ready to get back on the canal. As the last of the railroad ties were loaded, Father called me on deck and pointed to a boat moored in the boat basin.

"Finn, isn't that the boat that was behind us in the river gorge two days ago?" he asked.

I only needed a quick glance to recognize it.

"Yes, Father, it is," I replied. "It's the boat with the disrespectful captain."

"Those men look a little green in the face, like they're sick from something," Father observed. "You don't think it was the bear meat, do you?"

"I hope so," I said, raising Father's eyebrows a bit. "It serves them right. It's just a part of the way the world works."

"The way the world works?" Father said. "What do you mean?"

"I'm not sure, Father. I'm just trying to figure out something an old woman in Freemansburg told me. That's all."

"Well, keep thinking about it," Father said. "It's good to try to understand the world. Right now our world is taking us to Mauch Chunk. We better be on our way."

The trip back to Mauch Chunk was the

same as the trip up: twenty-nine locks, twenty dams, and twenty-six miles. We passed a spot not far downriver from White Haven where the water was an odd shade of black. There were buildings along the river and huge piles of tree bark. Men were unloading animal hides from wagons and carrying them into the buildings.

I noticed the river was littered with dead fish near the buildings. They were floating belly up near pipes that emptied into the river. My stone began to feel warm again, which didn't surprise me. It seemed to do that whenever I saw something in nature that was in trouble.

"What is that place, Father?" I said.

"It's a tannery, Finn, a place where animal hides are made into leather. There are lots of them along the Lehigh River and other streams. There's a large one in Bethlehem operated by the Moravian people."

My Indian stone cooled as we floated past the tannery. I thought about the fish and the black water and felt the two must be connected somehow.

We spent the rest of the day winding our way down the river gorge, dropping through one huge lock after another. We arrived in Mauch Chunk at eight o'clock in the evening. There were canal boats moored everywhere. Conan and Rogan towed the *Belfast Queen* to a large boat basin at the lower end of town, and we sat in the cabin to eat. Father told us his plans for the next day.

"Men who work for a rich railroad man named Asa Packer are coming tomorrow to unload the ties," he said. "When they're finished, we'll start loading cargo for our next stop in Catasauqua. I'm having some large stoves loaded and a lot of iron rope. We're also taking coal.

"Colin, you'll help load the boat. Finn, I'd like you to go to the mule barn and brush and feed the mules. You'll get a chance to see Mauch Chunk in the daylight, just as you wanted."

"Father, may I have five cents of my pay?" I asked. "I might see some candy I can buy for Colin and me."

Father smiled. "Certainly, Finn, you have earned it. Here are five pennies. Please don't lose them."

The next morning I was off to explore Mauch Chunk. The town was nestled in mountains that rose almost straight up from the Lehigh River. Canal boats were moored all along the river and it seemed every one of them was being loaded with hard, black coal. I saw lots of houses and stores and a huge hotel called the Mansion House. It was five levels tall. I saw a beautiful church called

St. Mark's and the factories that made the stoves and iron rope that Father was having loaded on the *Belfast Queen*.

I passed a shop where a newspaper called the *Mauch Chunk Gazette* was printed. The daily edition was displayed in the shop's front window. The biggest headline was about a telegraph line being built from the Mississippi River to the Pacific Ocean. There was a smaller headline about a "Farmer's High School" opening in the middle of Pennsylvania, and another about Chief Seattle's speech. I didn't know who Chief Seattle was, but I wanted to have Father read the story to me, so I went into the shop and bought a copy of the paper for two pennies.

Near the print shop was a bank that had red, white and blue banners on the front and a big sign that read "Open for Business!" Painted across the bank's large glass windows were more words that read "Mauch Chunk Bank." I looked closer and saw iron bars behind the glass.

"Do you think robbers could get in there?" a voice behind me asked.

I was caught by surprise. I turned around to see a boy my size just an arm's length away. He had red hair, a face full of freckles and a peppermint stick in his mouth. I noticed his right hand only had four fingers.

"Who are you, and why did you sneak up on me like that?" I asked.

"I'm John Gorman," he said. "I live in Summit Hill but I visit Mauch Chunk a lot. I never saw you here before, so I thought I'd come over and say hello."

"John Gorman?" I said. "Why, my name is Finn Gorman. I'm glad to meet you, John. I'm only here for a day. My father is at the boat basin with our canal boat. Would you like to meet him?"

"Sure, Finn," he said. "I'd like to meet anyone named Gorman."

It was a meeting that would lay the foundation for a long friendship. John and I talked all the way back to the boat basin. He took me to the best candy shop in town and I came back with peppermint sticks and molasses taffy, which pleased Colin immensely. The shop had boxes of Whitman's chocolates, but the three pennies I had weren't enough to buy them.

"Father!" I shouted as I approached the boat. "I want you to meet my new friend. His name is John Gorman."

Father turned quickly to see who I brought with me.

"Why, hello lad," Father said to John. "Your name is Gorman?"

"Yes, sir," John replied. "I mentioned to Finn that maybe we're related. My father works at a coal mine in Summit Hill. Can you come visit him and my mother?"

"Ah, I wish I could," Father said. "But I have a full day here. We are leaving early in the morning for Catasauqua. I'm sorry, lad, but I'll have to meet your father and mother another time."

My mouth opened as soon as Father's closed.

"I can go," I said. "I promise to brush and feed the mules. Please, Father, I want to see a coal mine and I have to know if John and I are related."

"How will you get there, Finn?" Father asked. "We don't have a wagon and John doesn't have a horse." I felt my plan was about to end. Then John spoke up.

"Mr. Gorman, Finn and I can ride to Summit Hill on the railroad we call the Switchback," he said. "I know the men who operate it. We'll ride in an empty coal car to Summit Hill and come back in a full one. I do it all the time. Finn will be back before dark."

I looked at Father and he looked at me. "The Switchback railroad," he said. "Is it safe, John?"

"Yes, sir, very safe," John answered. "No one has ever gotten hurt."

"Alright, Finn, you may go," Father said. "It would be nice to know if we are related to John's family, and I think it would be good for you to see a coal mine.

"But take care of the mules first."

Hooray! I had a new friend with the same last name and I was going to ride a railroad to a mining town. I thanked Father and gave him a hug.

"Come on, Finn, we better get going," John said. "The cars will be leaving Mauch Chunk soon."

After I brushed the mules, we ran back into town and headed for the Switchback. An exciting day was about to begin.

CHAPTER 17

A WONDERFUL RIDE

My day on the Switchback with John Gorman was one of the most memorable days of my life. I remember every detail.

John took me up Susquehanna Street to Broadway, a narrow road that followed Mauch Chunk Creek into the mountains west of town. I looked behind me across the Lehigh River and marveled at the size of a round mountain that rose above the canal.

"That's Bear Mountain," John said. "That's what Mauch Chunk means in Indian language. People say an Indian warrior named Onoko killed a sleeping bear there. Then he and his wife, Wenonah, were killed by a great spirit that wanted revenge for the bear. I like stories like that.

"That town at the bottom of Bear Mountain is East Mauch Chunk. You'll have a better view of it soon."

We started climbing a hill and walked past a large house that John said was once owned by a man named Josiah White. John told me that Mr. White designed the Lehigh Canal and a lot of other things including the Switchback.

"There's the ticket house," John said as we approached a small building farther up the hill. "That's where we get on the Switchback. The men there know me. All we have to do is climb into one of the empty coal cars and wait for the barney car to start things off."

I had never done anything quite so adventurous. Traveling on the *Belfast Queen* and sitting in a lumber camp wagon seemed ordinary compared to what I was about to do.

John was right. I did have a good view of East Mauch Chunk and Bear Mountain from the ticket house, but I had an even better view of a mountain looming to my left. It made Bear Mountain look downright puny. Right smack in the middle of it was the Switchback railroad. It went almost straight up. I felt a certain queasiness in my stomach.

"What do you think of that, Finn?" John asked me. I didn't answer.

"Finn, I said what do you think of the Switchback?"

"Do we have to go up that mountain?" I asked, already knowing the answer.

"Sure, that's one of the best parts," John said. "That's Mt. Pisgah, the tallest mountain around these parts. Then a while later we get to go up Mt. Jefferson. That's near my home in Summit Hill."

"Are you certain this is safe?" I asked. "Those railroad paths are pretty steep. What if the car doesn't make it, or starts to slide backwards."

"The cars can't slide backwards," John said. "They built cat steps to prevent that. Once we start going up, we won't stop until we reach the engine house at the top. See it up there? Then we glide down all the way to Mt. Jefferson. It's about six miles. And Finn, those paths are called tracks. They're railroad tracks."

"Look, Finn, here comes the barney car. Let's get ready to go. Climb into the front car."

I looked behind me and saw a strange-looking wooden car coming out of an underground pit. It had two wide iron straps attached to the front and was being pulled up a set of narrow iron rails. Ahead of it was a line of eight empty coal cars.

"Come on, Finn, jump in," John urged me. "Once the barney touches the last car in the line, we'll start to go up the mountain."

"What's pulling the barney car?" I asked John as I climbed into the front coal car.

"There's a big steam engine in the house at the top of the mountain," he replied. "It powers a big wheel that holds the barney car's iron straps. When the wheel turns, it rolls up the straps and pulls the barney up the mountain. Then the barney pushes all the cars in front of it up the mountain. I've heard the engine is as powerful as ninety horses."

All of a sudden I felt our car begin to move. I gripped the sides until my knuckles turned white. Then I closed my eyes. John looked at me and started laughing.

"Finn," he said. "Your name is Gorman. If you and I are related, then I know you're brave. Open your eyes and enjoy the ride."

"Alright," I said. "I will." And from that moment on, I decided I was going to have fun, no matter how scary the ride became.

I looked behind us and saw a man in the coal car at the back of the line.

"He operates the brakes when we go downhill," John said. "I see it's Mr. Sherman today. He lets the cars go faster than most brakemen."

Good gracious, I thought. Just my luck.

The ride up Mt. Pisgah was a real treat. I looked all around as we climbed. Behind us were the Lehigh River and the canal. The canal boats looked tiny from the mountain and the town's buildings looked like little wooden toys. We kept climbing until I could hear the engine working inside the engine house. I was amazed at how easily it pulled us up the hill.

The top half of the engine house was built in an arch over the tracks. As we passed through I felt like I was on top of the world. We were higher than anything else; I could see miles and miles in any direction.

"This is wonderful!" I shouted to John. "Where do we go next?"

"We go downhill to Mt. Jefferson," he said. "Look in front of you; we're ready to go over the trestle."

A gorge in the mountain loomed in front of us. It was about forty feet deep and more than two hundred feet wide. Built over it was a wooden trestle that carried the Switchback.

"Will it hold us?" I asked John. He just laughed. If the trestle cracked, we were goners. I held my breath as we went over and refused to look down. John laughed even harder. I guess whoever built that trestle knew what they were doing, because we cruised over it without so much as a shimmy or shake. I breathed a giant sigh of relief.

Nothing was pushing us anymore. From here on, we went downhill by force of gravity. We were on top of the mountain ridge and descending at an easy rate of speed. Mr. Sherman told us we were traveling about ten miles an hour.

It wasn't long before we reached a place called "Five Mile Tree," where we crossed a short bridge that spanned a set of tracks below us.

"We'll be going back to Mauch Chunk on those tracks," John told me. "And a little faster than now."

Mt. Jefferson rose about a mile in front of us. We came to a stop at the bottom and once again got pushed to the top by a barney car. We rode through another engine house and made an easy glide into Summit Hill. John and I jumped out and waved good-bye to Mr. Sherman. In a few minutes we were at John's home.

CHAPTER **18**

BREAKER BOYS

"Mother! Mother!" John yelled as we approached his house in Summit Hill. "I've brought someone from Mauch Chunk."

A slender woman with long reddish hair walked out of the house. She shielded her eyes from the sun and appeared quite curious to see who her son had brought home.

"Mother, this is Finn Gorman," John said. "He's from downriver near Bethlehem. His father is a boat captain and they came to Mauch Chunk on business. Did you hear his last name, Mother? It's Gorman!"

"Yes, John," Mrs. Gorman said. "I did indeed. Come in, Finn. Welcome to our home. John seems quite excited to have you here."

"Yes, ma'am," I replied, "I'm excited, too. I think we could be related."

"Perhaps we are, Finn," Mrs. Gorman chuckled. "Let's sit down and talk. I'd like to learn more about you and your family."

I told John's mother everything I could remember: the potato famine in Ireland; the trip across the Atlantic Ocean; living in New York, and coming to Pennsylvania and Free-mansburg. Mrs. Gorman listened patiently and never interrupted my story.

"Finn, we came here from Ireland, too," she said when I was done. "My husband was a coal miner in a little town called Arigna, in County Roscommon. The potato famine affected us, too, like it did your family. We left by ship from Dublin. Young John was a baby like you when we came over. I had another son, just like your mother has Colin, but he died on the way over. The trip across the ocean was too much for him.

"My husband, Seamus, refused to live in New York. There were gangs of thieves and thugs that roamed the streets and hurt people. They were always asking for money, but we had none to give them.

"We came directly to Pennsylvania after Mr. Gorman heard about the coal mines. He started as a laborer and never received a promotion. He is honest and works hard, but he's Irish, and a lot of people in these parts don't like us Irish. Mr. Gorman nor any of the other Irish workers in the mine will ever get a promotion. The bosses love the men as workers, but don't have much respect for them as people. But without the Irish, the mines would never produce coal, because no one else would do such dangerous work for so little pay.

"Look at poor John," she continued. "He lost a finger during an accident at the breaker house when he was only eight years old. His father will not let him return. He is one of the few boys in Summit Hill who doesn't work at the colliery or in the coal mine."

"Father wants me to get a good education, so I don't have to work in the coal mine when I get older," John said. "My friends are all breaker boys. They work twelve to fifteen hours a day, with only a short break for lunch. They cut their hands and break their fingers and sniff in coal dust until they cough. Some of them get sick but still have to work.

"And they only get paid a few pennies a day." John added. "They don't like it but they have to work because their fathers don't earn enough money for their families to survive. We survive because Mother spends a few hours each day at the mine owner's house cooking for his family. She doesn't get paid much, but it's a help."

John was anxious to take me to the mine. I thanked Mrs. Gorman and the next second John and I were off like a shot for the Switchback. When we got there, a line of empty coal cars was about to be pushed down a track headed for the Panther Valley.

"Mr. Finney, can we jump in?" John shouted to a man working next to the track.

"Sure, John," he called back. "Going to see your father, are you?"

"Yes, sir, Mr. Finney," John said. "I'll tell him you said hello."

We jumped into a car just as it began to move. After a couple of miles, we came to a little village called Ashton. John asked Mr. Finney to slow the cars so we could jump out. My attention was drawn to an ear-splitting noise coming from a tall wooden building near the railroad track. The noise was so loud that it shook the building.

"What is that place?" I asked John.

"It's the colliery," he said. "Most people call it the breaker house. It's where my friends work and it's also where I lost my finger. Coal from the mine is taken in there and crushed with huge hammers. That's why it's so noisy."

"Can we go in?" I asked.

"No," John said without hesitating. "The boss in there wouldn't like that. But we can peek in. Come with me, and be quiet."

The air near the breaker house was filled with black dust. I coughed and John gave me a handkerchief to put over my mouth and nose. We climbed on top of some wooden crates and peeked through a small, dirty window. I couldn't believe what I saw.

There were thirty to forty young boys inside sitting on little wooden planks. They were as crummy as could be, their clothes and hands and faces covered with thick black soot. Most of them wore handkerchiefs over their noses and mouths so they wouldn't breathe in the black dust that filled the air. The planks they sat on were arranged in neat rows over narrow wooden chutes that carried coal and other rocks that were crushed at the top of the breaker. They were all hunched over; no one looked from side to side. In the middle of everyone stood a nasty looking man holding a thick stick.

"*Shhhh*," John whispered. "That's the breaker boss. If one of those boys slows down or talks, the boss will hit him with that stick."

The breaker boys' job was to separate coal from waste rock, which John called culm. They'd let the coal slide down the chutes but when a piece of culm came by, they'd lower their feet into the chute to slow the whole pile. Then they'd pick out the culm and toss it into another chute that took it outside. The coal kept going and was sorted according to size. The boys' hands were in awful condition, but no one wore gloves. If they did, they wouldn't be able to pick up the culm as fast and the boss would hit them for being too slow. Most of the boys were my age and even younger.

"I think I've seen enough of this place," I told John. "Can we meet your father?"

We jumped to the ground and ran to the mine. I don't know what I was expecting, but all I saw was a dark tunnel. I looked down but it was pitch black; I couldn't see anything. All of a sudden a mule came out of the tunnel pulling a cart full of coal. I jumped back. Behind him was a man holding a whip and wearing a hat on his head that held a tiny lighted lantern.

"Is the mine down there?" I asked John.

"Of course it is," he laughed. "Mines aren't dug on top of the ground. That tunnel goes down hundreds of feet, and it goes off in all different directions."

"Is that all the light they have?" I said.

"There are a few bigger lanterns, too," John replied. "But they still don't give off a lot of light. If your lantern goes out, you can't see your hand in front of your face. It's scary. Sometimes there are explosions down there if a lantern is lighted in a gas pocket. Then you have cave-ins. There are rats all over the place, too."

As I was watching the mule pull the cart of coal, a second man walked out of the tunnel. He was tall with a broad mustache and pleasant smile. I knew immediately it was Mr. Gorman. He had an uncanny resemblance to Father. John introduced me and quickly told my story.

"So, lad, you think we might be relatives," Mr. Gorman said. "It would be a fine thing, wouldn't it?"

"Yes, sir, it would," I said. "I'd like to bring my family here some day."

"And I'd like to meet them," Mr. Gorman replied. "I'm sure we'd have much to talk about. I hope to see you again, Finn, but now it's time for me to return to work."

Mr. Gorman shook my hand and John and I jumped into a car full of coal that was being pulled to the Switchback and then on to Mauch Chunk. The sun was getting lower in the sky. It was time I got back to the *Belfast Queen*.

Mrs. Gorman was standing next to the railroad as we passed through Summit Hill. I waved and shouted to her that I would be back. As we left town, we passed a spot where the ground was smoking. The air smelled like rotten eggs.

"That's Burning Mine," John said. "It's been burning underground for years. No one knows when it will stop. There's always smoke and that foul smell. Hold on, Finn, the ride is going to get good. We should be in Mauch Chunk in about thirty minutes."

"Thirty minutes?" I questioned, thinking John was joking. "It took us three hours to get here."

"I know," he said, "but now it's all downhill. Hold onto your hat."

Our line of eight cars was heavy with coal, and they had no problem gaining speed whenever the brakeman allowed. The coal shook and created clouds of black dust as we rumbled over the track. This was totally different than being pushed uphill by a barney car.

"I'll wager we're going forty miles an hour," John yelled. I didn't answer. I just prayed we wouldn't go any faster.

I could hear the brakeman laughing above all the noise of the cars. Listening to him, I feared my prayers would not be answered. Then I looked ahead and saw nothing but a long straight line of track.

"We're on the home stretch!" John screamed. "It's two miles of straight track. Isn't this great?"

All I could think about was the disrespectful boat captain and how green his face became after

he ate the bear meat. I was sure that right now my face was much greener than that. Finally I yelled at the top of my lungs.

"WHEN DO WE GET TO MAUCH CHUNK?"

And with that, the cars slowed down to a gradual, pleasing stop. In front of me were the great coal chutes of Mauch Chunk. Behind me was a memory I would hold onto for more than one reason.

"I hope you liked the ride, Finn," John said. "We can do it again the next time you come here."

I smiled and nodded my head. My face was black from coal soot and I was as wobbly as a duck. I took a deep breath, shook the dust from my clothes and walked over to John.

"Thank you, John," I said. "This was the most marvelous day of my life. And the scariest."

We bent over laughing. John and I were both Gormans, but better than that, we had become true friends. I knew I would see him again. I walked back to the boat basin and told Father and Colin my story. It was a good day, one I would never forget.

CHAPTER 19
IRON PIGS FOR MR. KNECHT

Rain fell on and off the next day as we traveled from Mauch Chunk to Catasauqua. Colin's bare feet were coated with brown mud and the mules' soggy hats were constantly draped over their eyes. I knew Colin wished he had shoes. It sure was dreary.

With thirty-five locks ahead of us, there wasn't enough time to get to Catasauqua in one day. We pulled into the boat basin at Lockport the first night, right next to the Lockport Hotel. A lot of captains ate supper there, but since we were trying to "pinch pennies," I made a meal on the cabin stove.

The hotel was the nicest building in Lockport. Mr. Beck, the owner, also had a boat business and blacksmith shop. Our mules' shoes were holding up well, so Conan and Rogan didn't have to visit Mr. Beck's smithy. The only things they needed were food and water and some grass to roll on and scratch their backs.

We were on the canal one week. Colin and I started to trade jobs, which gave me a chance to stretch my legs and Colin time to rest his feet. Father never stopped the boat when we switched. He'd steer toward the bank and I'd use the boat pole to vault to the towpath. Colin would pick it up and vault onto the boat. We got good at it and had a lot of fun.

We left Lockport at four o'clock the next morning. By now I was blowing the conch shell and lighting the nighthawker. If we ran out of meal supplies, it was my job to vault to shore and barter with a locktender's wife for fresh vegetables or eggs or meat. Sometimes she wanted money instead of coal, so Father always made sure I had ten or twelve pennies.

After I got my supplies, I'd run down the towpath to catch our boat. Father tossed me the pole as the *Belfast Queen* hugged the bank, and I'd sling the sack of supplies across my back and vault onto the deck. I got pretty good at it, although I'd usually break an egg or two.

Rain was still falling when we reached Catasauqua. We dropped through Lock 36 and Father moored the boat and walked into an office building next to the canal. There was a sign on it that read "Crane Iron Company".

Lots of other boats were moored with us, each with a full load of coal. The boats were so heavy with coal and so low in the water that it looked like they might sink. All of this coal was going to be burned in the Crane iron furnaces. It burned long and it burned real hot. It was a much better fuel than the charcoal that iron furnaces used before.

Father returned from the office and informed us that once the *Belfast Queen* was unloaded, it would be reloaded with Crane iron headed to Mr. Knecht's foundry in Shimersville. He said we were going to have a boat full of iron pigs.

"Iron pigs," Colin laughed. "What are they?"

Father chuckled, too. "Iron pigs are what the workers call the iron bars made here," he said. "Let's walk to the furnace buildings while our boat is being unloaded. Maybe we can see some pigs being roasted."

Colin and I made little oinking noises as we walked toward the furnaces. We giggled at ourselves. Father just shook his head. I looked up at the grey, cloudy sky and saw black smoke and orange flames bellowing from a furnace stack that towered above everything. A wide wooden platform at the top of the stack held two men who pushed coal and iron ore and other rocks down the opening. Every time they dumped something they jumped back as fast as they could to get away from the heat and smoke. Watching them made me glad I worked on a canal boat.

I saw five or six stacks along the canal. Each one had a huge brick building attached to it that Father called a casting house. That's where the iron pigs were made.

We walked through the mud toward the closest casting house. Large wagons pulled by teams of horses or mules waited outside. Each wagon was loaded with iron ore from nearby mines. The drivers sat in the rain, waiting their turn to unload. Crews of workers dressed in long leather aprons and heavy gloves and boots stood outside the casting house doors. We were given permission to enter if we stayed as far away from the furnace as possible.

As soon as we stepped inside I was hit by hot, dry air. The walls glowed yellowish-orange near the furnace but the rest of the building was dim, almost dark in some corners. An obnoxious odor

filled the room. I put my handkerchief over my mouth and nose but it didn't help. Workers were pushing carts and lifting iron bars and tending the monster furnace. It was hard, hot, sweaty work.

"The pigs are made next to the furnace," Father shouted above all the noise. "The coal fire in the furnace gets so hot that it melts the iron out of the iron ore. The melted iron sinks to the bottom of the furnace. When enough collects, a worker opens a spout that lets the iron pour out.

Hot, melted iron, I thought. Why, it sounded like that volcano stuff called lava I'd read about in one of my school books. I never knew coal could get hot enough to melt other rocks.

"What happens then, Father?"

"The hot iron pours from the spout and runs down a long channel to a part of the casting house floor that's made of sand. The channel has openings on its sides that lead into rows of small troughs molded into the sand. The iron flows into those openings and fills the troughs. When the iron cools and gets hard, it takes the shape of the troughs. Some workers think the troughs look like little piglets suckling on a sow."

The piglets suckling Mr. Fritchman's sows back home didn't look anything like these. But at least I knew why the bars were called iron pigs.

The heat inside the building was tremendous. There were loud whooshing noises coming from the furnace that I did not like. As we turned to leave, I saw a boy sitting in a corner at the far end of the building. He looked lonely.

"Father, how much time is left until the boat is loaded with iron pigs?" I asked.

"Five or six hours," Father said. "And by that time, it will be too late for us to leave Catasauqua tonight. Why do you ask?"

I turned my head toward a corner of the building.

"Do you see that boy over there?" I asked. "I thought I'd walk over and say hello."

"It's fine with me if you want to talk," Father said, "but please don't leave the building unless you're coming back to the boat. Once it's loaded, we have to move it to a basin for the night."

"Thank you, Father," I said. "I won't get lost."

Colin and Father walked out of the casting house and I went toward the boy. When I got closer, I could see he was sleeping. His boots were caked with black mud and the legs of his trousers were wet. His jacket rested on him like a blanket; he had his hat pulled down over his eyes. I thought I'd make a little noise. Maybe it would wake him.

"Harrumph . . . harrumph." Nothing, not a movement.

"Harrumph!" Not a thing.

I bent over and shook his shoulder.

"Hello, are you awake?" I said. "I'm Finn Gorman. How are you?"

He lifted his chin and tilted his hat so he could see who was talking. He didn't look too happy that I had interrupted his sleep.

"Who are you?" he said. "What are you waking me for? Let me gather my wits." He yawned and pulled himself up in the corner.

I extended my hand.

"I'm Finn Gorman. I'm here with my Father and brother to unload coal and pick up iron pigs."

"Iron pigs?" the boy said. "Nobody here calls 'em iron pigs. They're just pigs. What did you say your name was?"

"Finn Gorman," I repeated. "I'm from Shimersville, near Bethlehem."

"Yeah, I know where it is," the boy said. "Sometimes Pa takes me to Bethlehem. We hitch rides on canal boats. My name is Daniel McCabe. You can call me Danny."

"Nice to meet you, Danny," I said. "I didn't know you were asleep. I thought you were bored being here by yourself. I figured I'd come over and say hello. We're staying in Catasauqua overnight."

While I was talking, Danny was looking at my neck. I didn't know why, so I didn't pay much attention. He said his father was a wagon driver for the Crane Iron Company and made three or four runs a day between company mines in the countryside and the furnaces in Catasauqua. Danny was inside the casting house staying dry and warm while his father's wagon was being unloaded in the rain.

"My Pa works real hard," Danny said. "We live in Catasauqua and drive to the mines outside town every day. On days like this the roads are nothing but thick mud. Wagons get stuck and mules slip and get hurt. Sometimes the wagons roll over and the whole load of ore gets dumped in the mud. The new plank road helps, but it's always being repaired.

"People are opening mines around here as fast as they're laying claims for gold in California and Alaska," Danny continued, describing the land around Catasauqua and Siegfried's Bridge.

"There are underground mines and pit mines and big quarries for limestone. The countryside lost its trees years ago. They were cut and burned into charcoal for the old iron furnaces. Thank goodness these Crane furnaces use coal or there wouldn't be trees left anywhere. We'd have a great sea of mud like Pa and I drove through today."

"How long have you driven with your father?" I asked Danny.

"Well, I'm thirteen and I started when I was nine, so I guess that makes three years," he said.

"No," I replied. "It makes four."

"It does?" Danny asked, a bit miffed. "Are you a genius?"

"No, I'm no genius. I just like to do numbers in my head, that's all," I replied. "Do you go to school?"

"I wish I did, but I can't," Danny said. "I have to work with Pa every day. The company works

73

him seven days a week. He hardly ever gets a day off. I'm with him as much as I can, and it doesn't leave time for school. We barely survive on Pa's pay. Ma has me and four younger ones. I could get a job doing something, but Pa would miss my help. I know it's worth more to him to have me there."

Danny began looking at my neck again. Finally, his curiosity got the best of him. "What's attached to that leather string around your neck?"

Other kids I met often wondered the same thing. I never gave anyone much of an answer, but I decided to say more to Danny.

"It's my Indian stone," I told him. "I found it on our property and I think it's special. I think it has powers. This stone gets real warm, even hot, when I see something in the natural world that's not right. A boat captain shot a bear in the river gorge a few days ago and the stone nearly burned my chest.

"The first time it happened I thought I was just imagining things. But then it happened again and again. I feel it's trying to tell me something, or warn me of something before it happens."

"I wish I had a stone like that," Danny said. "Is it warm now?"

"Everything in here is warm," I said. "But not the stone."

I sat down. Danny and I watched a man take a hammer and break the clay cork on the furnace spout. The glowing light from the melted iron made us squint our eyes. We watched it flow down the channel.

"They're making pigs," Danny said.

"Iron pigs," I replied. "Iron pigs for Mr. Knecht."

CHAPTER

BACK TO SCHOOL

I was anxious to see Mother and little Rose. Freemansburg was only seven locks away. Colin and I figured we'd be there by mid-afternoon.

Catasauqua disappeared behind us as we began our tow. I cleaned the breakfast dishes and brought Father a cup of coffee.

"Finn," he told me as he sipped, "you've been a mighty big help on this trip. You and your brother have proven that I have the best crew on the canal."

"Thank you, Father," I said. "I've had fun. I'm looking forward to the rest of the trip."

"I'll bet you're also looking forward to a day in school, aren't you?" Father asked.

"I am, Father. I miss my friends."

"Which school will you attend tomorrow?" he asked.

Hmmm. I had two choices. I could stay in Shimersville or ride to the Franklin School with Jennie and her uncle.

"I think I'm going to go to Franklin School, Father," I said. "I like the teacher there." I never

told Father that sitting next to Jennie on the wagon had something to do with my decision, although he may have been able to figure that out himself.

We dropped through Lock 43 and entered Freemansburg at two o'clock. Everything looked the same.

"Finn!" Father called.

"Yes, sir?"

"Finn, when you're done with your jobs, I have one more for you. I just paid your brother his wages for the trip and he took off like a shooting star for Mr. Moser's shoe shop. Would you ride home and tell your mother we're here?"

"YES, SIR!"

I never unharnessed a mule so fast. Within minutes, Conan and I were off to our hill above Shimersville. That mule didn't need me to tell him where to go. We were across the wooden bridge and turning into our property in no time. Conan pulled up in front of the house and I jumped off.

"Mother, I'm home!" I yelled.

Little Rose came out the front door and put her arms around me, something she avoided before. I heard a tin pot fall in the kitchen, followed by Mother's happy voice.

"Finn, I'm so glad you're home! Let me see you." Mother came outside and gave me a hug I'll never forget.

"Where are your Father and Colin?" she asked.

"Down at the basin, Mother. Mr. Knecht and his workers are coming to unload iron pigs from the *Belfast Queen*. Father told me to let you know we're here."

I never saw a person move so fast as Mother did that moment. She whisked little Rose into her arms and within minutes we were off to the boat basin. Mother and Father were happy to see each other and talked all the way home and for hours after supper. There was a lot of news to share.

I slept well that night and woke at the crack of dawn to do my chores and meet my ride to school.

Jennie's uncle drove her to the Franklin School at the same time every day. If I was standing along the road when they passed, he'd stop and pick me up.

I liked school. I learned wonderful things and got to play tag and hoops and marbles on the schoolyard after lunch. Sometimes if we had enough kids, we'd go to the field next to the school and play a new game called baseball. All we needed was a yarn ball and a sturdy stick to hit it.

There were a lot of boys and girls at the school from surrounding farms. Their parents were German and they didn't speak English. In order to learn the language, the kids had to attend a public school. Mr. Nimsch, our teacher, grew up in a part of Germany called Saxony. He spoke both languages, so he was perfect for the job. When he was teaching a lesson in German, kids like me who spoke English would read books or do homework.

Sometimes Mr. Nimsch would ask me to go outside and bring in wood that he split in the morning, or coal if we had some. Either fuel burned in the potbelly stove that heated the school. If we needed drinking water, one of the students would take a bucket to the outside pump. Sometimes in winter when the pump froze up, we'd collect snow or ice and melt it on the stove.

Franklin School wasn't large, just one big room, but it held all the local kids who were old enough for grades one to eight. It was made of stone and wood and had five sides. Some schools had large bells to call students inside for lessons. Franklin School didn't have one, so Mr. Nimsch bought a large hand bell that he rang in the morning and after lunch. When we heard it, we knew it was time to stop playing and begin learning.

There weren't enough desks, so some of the little kids shared. The seat was long enough for two first- or second-graders, or even third-graders if they were skinny. The top of each desk had a

hole for an ink well. Since paper was so scarce and expensive, we did most of our lessons on slate boards. We shared small ones at our desks or stood and wrote on big boards attached to the walls. We wrote with slate pencils, but for handwriting lessons and journals, Mr. Nimsch gave us paper and ink and a pen made from a goose or turkey quill. It was fun making fancy letters with ink.

Every day started with the Lord's Prayer and a Bible reading. Kids who were talking or not paying attention got a good tap on the shoulder from Mr. Nimsch's switch. He had a favorite tree on the edge of the schoolyard that supplied them. Sometimes kids got switched a second time at home if they had a brother or sister in school who was a tattletale.

Mr. Nimsch had a big dictionary next to his desk. If someone didn't know what a certain word meant, he would tell them to visit the dictionary. If they didn't know how to use the dictionary, they received an individual lesson.

"Knowing what words mean and how to spell them are the keys to good reading," Mr. Nimsch was fond of saying. "The dictionary is your friend."

While there was only one dictionary, we had other books to use in school or at home if we took good care of them. My favorites were the McGuffey spelling and reading books and *McNally's Geography*. It introduced me to so many places around the world. Mr. Nimsch allowed the older kids to borrow some of his personal books. Colin enjoyed reading *Moby Dick*, even though it took him a long time. He said it was a great adventure about a ship captain named Ahab and his quest to find a white whale.

Mr. Nimsch's favorite was *Arabian Nights*. He liked reading it to us following afternoon recess. The German kids couldn't understand everything, but heaven help their shoulders if they fell asleep while Mr. Nimsch was reciting. There were stories in the book about a boy named Ali Baba, a sailor named Sinbad, and a boy named Aladdin, who flew magic carpets and talked to a genie who lived in a magical lamp. I never got tired of listening.

A lot of kids around Shimersville and Freemansburg couldn't get to school because they were needed on the farm or canal. I was now one of those kids, but I read books both at home and aboard the *Belfast Queen* and kept up with my assignments. When the canal froze and was shut down around Thanksgiving, I went to school every day unless the snow was well above my knees. I knew Mr. Nimsch would be there to teach anyone who arrived.

My day at Franklin School was almost over. The sun was dipping and soon Jennie's uncle would arrive with his wagon. The third grade arithmetic lesson was almost over. They spent the whole year working with the numbers one to twelve. They added, subtracted, divided and multiplied those numbers in every way possible, over and over until there was no possible way they could forget. I remember doing that. It's probably why my head had all the answers whenever I had to calculate something.

Mr. Nimsch closed his lesson book at half past three o'clock and told us to enjoy our evening. Jenny's uncle took us back to Shimersville on Applebutter Road. On the way we passed wagon after wagon loaded with fruits and vegetables and hay. Jennie's uncle stopped his horse in front of our property and I jumped from the wagon.

"I'll see you another day, Jennie," I told my friend. "Father and I are delivering fruit and vegetables to Easton tomorrow. I probably won't be back in school for another week."

"That's alright, Finn," Jenny replied. "I know your father needs you on his boat. My father says he's becoming a fine boat captain. I'll help you with the lessons you miss."

Jennie's uncle snapped the horse's reins. I waved goodbye and the wagon disappeared around the bend. I knew I would see her another day.

HIGH SOCIETY

The autumn harvest was at its peak and Freemansburg was a hub of activity. Farmers from all over Lower Saucon and Bethlehem townships brought wagon loads of fruit and vegetables to the canal for shipment to towns and cities along the Lehigh and Delaware canals.

Father had arranged for the *Belfast Queen* to haul produce to Easton, which was only ten miles away. I had been there many times, mostly on Sundays when we worshiped at St. Bernard's Church, the only Catholic church in the Lehigh Valley.

I had a friend in Easton named Jimmy Reilly who lived on the outskirts of the city and attended St. Bernard's school. When Jimmy's school day was over, he helped paint the office of the new *Easton Daily Express* on North Fourth Street. The *Daily Express* was almost ready to begin publishing the city's only daily newspaper.

Jimmy's bosses – Mr. Eichman and Mr. Davis – were determined to make the *Daily Express* the best newspaper in the city. They even installed a telegraph machine on the third floor of the building to receive the latest news. No one else had one.

We left Freemansburg on Friday morning at nine o'clock, long after most of the other boats. The *Belfast Queen* was loaded with bushel upon bushel of apples and pears and peaches and tomatoes. Pumpkins and other large squashes covered a corner of the cargo area. There were sacks of corn meal and Irish potatoes and jugs of apple cider. Crocks full of fresh cheese and butter were stored on the bottom of the boat where it was cooler. I never saw so much food. All of it would be sold in Easton, where there were several grocery businesses and a huge Market House in Centre Square. Farmers from all over eastern Pennsylvania sold crops there.

The tow to Easton was easy and relaxing. The canal reflected the brilliant colors of the autumn leaves. Geese flew high above the Lehigh River in large V-shaped flocks, all heading in a southerly direction. I watched two boys set muskrat traps along the canal, hoping to catch some of the furry varmints that caused so many costly leaks. Each muskrat they caught would bring a bounty from the Lehigh Coal and Navigation Company.

We entered the river after dropping through Lock 46 at Hopesville. Conan and Rogan pulled us along the shoreline but then had to be ferried across the river at Smith's Island, where the canal switched from one side of the river to the other. We poled the boat across the river, met our mules on the other side and continued to Easton. We passed three large iron furnaces built next to the canal at a little village called Glendon. Father said we'd be there again in three days to load the boat with iron pigs.

We exited the canal at Lock 48 and entered the river one last time. We were just a stone's throw from Easton. I vaulted to the towpath to take the mules from Colin and unhitch them from the towline. After Colin vaulted onto the boat, I walked the mules down the towpath and across the Third Street Bridge into Easton. Father and Colin poled the *Belfast Queen* across the river and steered it into a basin where our cargo would be unloaded.

The day went quickly. Workers from Mr. Drake's grocery business arrived to unload the produce. We finished at three o'clock. After that, Father and I walked into the city, him to do business and me to see my friend Jimmy. Colin stayed with the boat and mules.

Easton was the largest town in the Lehigh Valley. It had more than seven thousand people, twice as many as Bethlehem and Allentown combined. If you added South Easton, there were more than nine thousand people.

"Places like Easton grow quickly," Father said as we neared North Fourth Street where the *Daily Express* was located. "Businessmen build factories here because they can ship their products anywhere on the canals and roads. The factories need workers and the workers need homes and places to shop. After a time, all the growth adds up and you have a town. That's what happened here."

I thought about that as we crossed North Fourth Street. Easton sure was different than any place I had seen. There was great wealth and a different type of culture, a kind of life some people called "high society."

Why, Easton was so important that Northampton County built its courthouse right in the middle of Centre Square. On any weekday you could see lawyers and politicians standing near the

courthouse in their fancy pants and coats and tall hats. Some of them carried shiny wooden canes and held the arms of ladies who were dressed as finely as queens.

My thoughts were interrupted by a familiar voice.

"Finn! Finn Gorman!"

It was Jimmy Reilly, standing on the corner of North Fourth and Church streets before he went upstairs to paint the newspaper office.

"Father, can I stay with Jimmy while you're doing business?" I asked. "We'll probably walk around town when he's done with his job."

"Certainly, Finn," Father replied. "Meet me at Centre Square at six o'clock and we'll head back to the boat. We'll be sleeping in Easton tonight."

"Thank you, Father," I said, and I was off to see my friend.

"Jimmy! How are you?" I yelled as I crossed North Fourth Street.

"Finn! Come on over."

I had to dodge a couple of carriages and a coal wagon, but I finally got across the street. Jimmy shook my hand and we spent the next several minutes catching up with each other's news. Jimmy was surprised that Father had bought a canal boat and that I was part of the crew. I wanted to know if there were any new stores to visit.

"There's a great new shop," Jimmy said. "It's called 'Eschenbach and Brothers French Confectionary and Fancy Tea Cake Bakers, Oyster and Ice Cream Saloon.' "

"What?" I said. "Well, don't repeat it; just tell me what it is."

"It's a place where they sell fancy pastries and cakes and ice cream," Jimmy explained. "And oysters."

I knew oysters were something like river mussels but I could not imagine why anyone would want to eat them with ice cream or fancy cakes. I liked ice cream all by itself.

"We'll walk there when I'm done cleaning the office," Jimmy said. "I'll even buy us something."

I helped Jimmy clean and we finished in less than one hour. Without blinking an eye, we ran down the steps and were off in search of the land of oysters and ice cream and fancy cakes.

"Jimmy," I said as we crossed North Fourth Street. "Let's visit Eschenbach's a little later. I'd like to go to Zulich's Music Store to see if anyone is playing the piano."

"Okay," Jimmy replied. "Let's go!"

We raced down Church Street and were set to cross North Third Street when we almost ran into a herd of cows that were being driven through the middle of the city by two men and three boys. One of the boys appeared to be my age. As I was watching, the boy looked in my direction. I smiled and waved.

"Where are you going with those cows?" I shouted.

"My Pa and my uncle are taking them to New Jersey," he shouted back. "We're going to swim them across the Delaware."

"You're going to do what?" I shouted back.

"Swim them across the Delaware," the boy repeated. "Come on with us if you don't believe me."

Jimmy and I looked at each other. Music and ice cream could wait. This was too exciting to resist. We jumped into the middle of all the dust and commotion and introduced ourselves.

"I'm Finn Gorman and this is my friend, Jimmy Reilly," I yelled over the grunts and moos of the cows. "What's your name?"

"Samuel Miller," he said. "I'm very pleased to meet you."

"Where do you live, Sam?" I asked.

"Well, Pa and I and my brother Aaron live in Dutchtown," he said. "You know, it's in west Easton, up near Bushkill Creek. My Uncle Jacob and cousin David live in Buffalo, New York. They have a farm where they raise all these cows."

"How did these cows get here from Buffalo?" I asked Sam. "That's awful far away."

"Well, we walked 'em here," he answered. "Pa and I drove to Buffalo in our wagon and then helped Uncle Jacob bring them down. We're taking them across the Delaware to be sold in New Jersey. They fetch a good price. That's our business; we're drovers. Sometimes we help Uncle Jacob, and sometimes we drive animals for local farmers. Other people in Dutchtown do it, too."

We dodged a few tails and horns to get closer to Sam. One of the dang cows stepped on my foot just as I was getting a good position. I winced.

"You have to keep your eye on them all the time," Sam told me as I hopped toward him. "They don't know where they're going. It's up to me and my hickory stick to keep 'em in line."

Jimmy and I made sure we stayed close to Sam once we reached him. One false move and I'd have my other foot squashed. I was amazed how only five people could keep a herd of more than one hundred cows in such a tight group.

Northampton County Courthouse was straight ahead of us. I saw some of the lawyers scurry toward the safety of the building. Farmers at the Market House pulled their produce closer to their tents.

"Keep them moving down Northampton Street," Sam's father shouted. "The river isn't far. Keep 'em moving or they'll eat the county's grass."

Everyone in Centre Square watched the spectacle as it paraded its way toward the broad Delaware. We passed Zulich's Music Store but I couldn't see if anyone was playing the piano because my vision was blocked by cow heads bobbing up and down.

We finally reached the Delaware River. Sam's father arranged to have a couple of men in boats swim the cows across the river. While we waited, we sat in the shade of a large sycamore tree and talked to Sam.

"I don't know anyone from Dutchtown," Jimmy told him. "Where do you go to school?"

"Well, I don't get to school too much because I'm always helping Pa," Sam said. "Sometimes I get to go to the Easton public school but most of my learning is done at the *Schul*."

"The what?" I said. "I don't know what that is."

"The *Schul* is a German school run by my synagogue. I go there on weekends when I'm home."

"What's a synagogue?" Jimmy asked. Poor Sam was getting asked a lot of questions.

"It's where I worship," Sam replied. "I'm Jewish, just like a lot of other German people in Dutchtown."

Well, I'd never met a Jewish person before and neither had Jimmy. Sam told us some things about his religion and we just figured it was another way for people to worship God. He told us some amazing stories about animal drives. One time he and his Pa were driving sheep from Buffalo to Easton and they had to wait five days to cross the Susquehanna River because it was flooded. Sam said he and his Pa had to keep an eye open for wolves while they took care of the sheep.

We were becoming comfortable in the shade when Sam's father gave the order to continue.

"Samuel, the cows are going into the river," he shouted. "It's time for us to cross the bridge."

85

The three of us got up and shook hands. I looked at the Delaware River and saw more than one hundred cows swimming in water up to their necks. They kept their heads high and straight and moved their legs as fast as they could. They swam just like dogs. A boatman rowed a small skiff on each side of the herd to keep the cows from going into fast water where they might drown. I'd never seen anything like it.

Sam and his relatives disappeared into the long covered bridge and Jimmy and I headed back up Northampton Street. Eschenbach's ice cream sounded even more delicious after our hot and dusty walk.

We passed Zulich's Music Store and, sure enough, there was a man sitting on a bench playing the most beautiful piano I had ever seen. We stopped and listened.

"That music sounds like it was written in heaven," I told Jimmy.

"It's a new piano, Finn," Jimmy said. "I haven't seen that one before. What does that sign next to it say?"

"Steinway, New York City," I replied. "A piano made in New York City. I bet it was brought in here on the Morris Canal."

A woman and young girl stood next to the piano. They seemed very interested.

"I'll bet that lady buys it," Jimmy said.

"But the sign says eight hundred dollars," I replied.

"That's nothing for some people in this city," Jimmy said. "How much do you think those homes on North Third Street cost? If they can afford those homes, they can sure afford a piano."

Jimmy was right. As soon as the man finished playing the piano, the woman shook his hand and reached into a small purse.

"I knew it! She's buying that Steinway piano from New York City. Wouldn't it be grand for us to have something like that, Finn?"

I agreed, but also knew it wasn't likely to happen unless we became rich like the high society people of Easton.

We continued on Northampton Street past Centre Square and finally arrived at "Eschenbach and Brothers French Confectionary and Fancy Tea Cake Bakers, Oyster and Ice Cream Saloon." I stared at the fancy lettering on the store window. Everything about the place seemed magical.

"What are you waiting for, Finn?" Jimmy asked. "Let's go in."

I felt awkward not having any money, but Jimmy really wanted to treat, so I asked for one scoop of vanilla.

"Take two," Jimmy insisted. "It's on me."

Our cold, sweet ice cream was gone all too soon. Before I knew, it was time to meet Father in Centre Square. As I walked back with Jimmy I glimpsed over my shoulder and saw the college called Lafayette overlooking the Delaware River. We passed Bixler's jewelry store and marveled at the precious gems on display inside. House after house had beautiful windows of colored glass and doors with shiny brass hinges and knobs. As we approached Centre Square I saw a man with a long pole lighting gas lamps that surrounded the courthouse. The bluish-yellow flames flickered slowly before they finally burst into a bright white light.

Then I saw Father, patiently waiting for me in front of White's Hotel. It had been a fine afternoon and I told Jimmy exactly that. We shook hands and Jimmy headed back up Northampton Street to his home on the west side of Easton.

On the way to the *Belfast Queen*, I told Father all about my day. Colin was waiting for us, patiently rubbing his new shoes with linseed oil. I walked onto the deck and went into the cabin. That night I dreamed of sharing vanilla ice cream with Jennie Geissinger at "Eschenbach and Brothers French Confectionary and Fancy Tea Cake Bakers, Oyster and Ice Cream Saloon." I hoped someday my dream would come true.

CHAPTER 22

SPIRIT OF THE FOREST

Any hope I had of sleeping late on Saturday morning abruptly disappeared two hours before the sun rose. Good gracious! Easton was awake and alive. Conch shells and horns blew everywhere. Coal tumbled loudly down wooden chutes at the loading docks behind us. Worst of all were the ear-splitting steam whistles that signaled the start of the day for hundreds of workers at the Abbot Street factories along the Lehigh River.

I pulled my feather pillow over my head and held it tight to my ears. "Father, will it stop soon?"

"No, Finn, it won't," he chuckled. "Easton doesn't sleep very long. Let's get up and have breakfast. We'll be heading home soon."

We had a quiet day ahead. Father's only responsibility was to stop at the furnaces in Glendon and arrange to pick up a load of iron pigs the following Monday. We would be hauling them to a town called New Hope along the Delaware Canal. I couldn't wait to see what another canal was like.

Conan and Rogan were happy to see me. I walked them across the South Easton bridge and met Colin and Father and the *Belfast Queen*. We were soon on our way and it

wasn't long before Father was at the Glendon iron furnaces making his plans.

Our stop was brief. Fifteen minutes later, I was on the mule ferry at Smith Island. Father and Colin poled the boat across the Lehigh one more time. A short tow along the river bank brought us to Lock 46 at Hopesville.

"Father," I said after we locked into the canal, "since I don't have any chores, can I walk home? It's not far."

"I suppose, Finn. Shall I tell Mother to expect you for lunch?"

"No. Maybe I'll stop at Geissinger's and see if Jennie is home."

"Alright, Finn, just be careful. And be home for supper."

I passed farms of all sizes as I walked the towpath from Hopesville to Freemansburg. I saw Augustus and Jonathan Shimer cutting corn and shaping it into shocks. Mr. Staller was loading huge orange pumpkins into his wagon. Everyone was taking advantage of the good autumn weather.

Ahead of me was Gwinner's Island, my favorite spot to look for Indian arrowheads. It was right across the river from Geissinger's grist mill. I took off my shoes and socks, rolled up my trousers and carefully picked my way across a shelf of rocks that stretched from the canal bank to the island. I made it without falling in.

I pulled on my socks and laced my shoes and started walking along the island's rocky edge, looking intently for stones of just the right size and shape. I was so focused on looking down that I never saw the sycamore limb hanging at forehead level in front of me.

"Ouch!" I moaned as I walked into it. "That hurt."

I heard a soft giggle. Good gracious, had someone seen me be so awkward? I looked up. There in front of me, not fifteen feet away, was a girl sitting on a large rock. She smiled and put a finger to her lips as though she wanted me to be quiet. Then she slowly stretched out an arm and pointed to a nearby log at the edge of the river.

I looked and saw a large turtle. It was black on top and kind of yellowish underneath. Its head was out of its shell and its eyes were closed. It was taking a nap in the warm afternoon sun.

The girl motioned me to join her. I turned and slowly walked toward her in a wide arc. I didn't want to disturb the turtle. I reached the rock and climbed up next to her.

She was dressed like any of the girls in Freemansburg, but her features were very different. She had long, shiny, coal black hair that was tied up behind her head. Her skin was very tan, almost bronze, and her cheekbones were prominent and gave a pleasant shape to her face. When she looked at me, I was captivated by her dark, smiling eyes.

"How is your forehead?" she whispered.

"Oh, it's alright," I answered. "That was kind of clumsy of me."

"What were you looking for?"

"Indian arrowheads," I replied. "I like to collect them. How long have you been watching that turtle?"

"An hour, maybe more," she said. "It was on the log when I arrived. I'll watch it until it decides to leave."

"What's your name?" I asked.

"Sarah. And yours?"

"I'm Finn Gorman, Sarah. Very pleased to meet you."

Sarah didn't provide her last name. She had a certain air of mystery about her, yet I felt very comfortable in her presence. I groped for something more to say but Sarah seemed content just watching the turtle bask in the sunshine. Then she broke the silence.

"Finn," she whispered. "The turtle has decided what it will do."

I looked at the log. As far as I could tell, the turtle was still asleep. It hadn't moved an inch. Then without notice its legs came out of its shell, it took three steps forward and eased itself into the river.

"How did you know it was going to move?" I said as we watched the turtle swim along the shoreline.

"The sun was no longer on its back," Sarah replied. "It was time to find another warm spot. A turtle is a patient creature, but once it makes up its mind, it always moves forward to a better situation."

Well, I had talked with Jennie about school and her father's business, and with Susan Dietrich about her father's canal boat, but I'd never had a conversation with a girl about animals, let alone turtles. Sarah seemed to know a lot.

I looked at her as she watched the turtle disappear downriver. I didn't know how Sarah came to be sitting on Gwinner's Island, or where she came from, but she certainly added interest to my day. A sudden gust of wind loosened her hair and blew it into her face. As she held it up to retie it, I noticed a thin strip of leather around her neck. I didn't want to seem rude, but I had to ask a question.

"What do you have around your neck, Sarah?"

She quickly buttoned the top of her blouse to hide the leather strip. She turned her head toward the river. I felt I had asked the wrong question. Then I had an idea. I reached underneath my shirt, grabbed my stone and pulled it over my head.

"Look, Sarah, here's what I wear around my neck."

She turned toward me and looked at the stone. Her dark eyes widened and her mouth opened. She was so still that I didn't know if she was breathing.

"Sarah, are you alright?" I asked.

"Where…where did you get that?" she said. "How long have you had it?"

"I found it this summer when my brother and I were training our mules," I answered. "It was buried in the ground behind our house. I thought it looked like a face. It had a hole in it, so I strung a strip of leather through it and started wearing it. It's done some strange things to me."

Sarah raised her hands and lifted the leather string off her neck and over her head. She held it in front of me. I could not believe what was tied to it.

"Sarah, it's my stone!" I said. "I mean it's your stone, but it's just like my stone."

Sure enough, it was identical in size, shape and color. It had the same indentations that looked like eyes and the same flat ridge that looked like a nose. Then Sarah said something I never expected.

"Finn, can I trust you to keep my secret? You are the only person I know who has a stone like mine. You must have it for a reason. Can I trust you to keep my secret?"

"Yes," I said without hesitation. "Yes, Sarah, you can trust me."

She held her stone tightly and looked at the sky. Her eyes closed and she took a deep breath. Then she spoke.

"Finn, I am Lenape *(Len-ah-pe),*" she said. "I am an Indian, and the stones we wear hold the spirit of Mesingw *(Mee-sing).* He is a powerful spirit who watches over animals and other living things of the forest. Those who carry the image of Mesingw receive the power of his spirit."

I was stunned. Not only was Sarah an Indian, but she was telling me that I was carrying a powerful spirit around my neck. The unusual sensations that angered and scared me during the last two weeks began to make sense. I had so many questions, but there was something I needed to know right away.

"Sarah, where do you live and how did you come to Gwinner's Island?"

"Finn, I trust you as a friend. Mesingw has chosen you, so I will tell you my story. I live near the Blue Mountain, in the land of my ancestors. My great-grandparents refused to leave their land when white settlers pushed most of our people west. They lived in secrecy to avoid conflict.

"My grandparents and parents also chose to stay in Lenapehocking *(Len-ah-pe-hock-ing),* the land of our forefathers. But it was difficult to avoid contact with white settlements, so they adopted the dress and language of the whites and lived quiet lives. Even though the Indian wars were long over, there were still many whites who would harm them in revenge.

"My parents died from disease when I was a little girl. My grandmother is raising me. I walk to this area to visit an uncle who lives nearby. I sit on this island and others in the river to observe the natural world and learn respect for the earth and its living things."

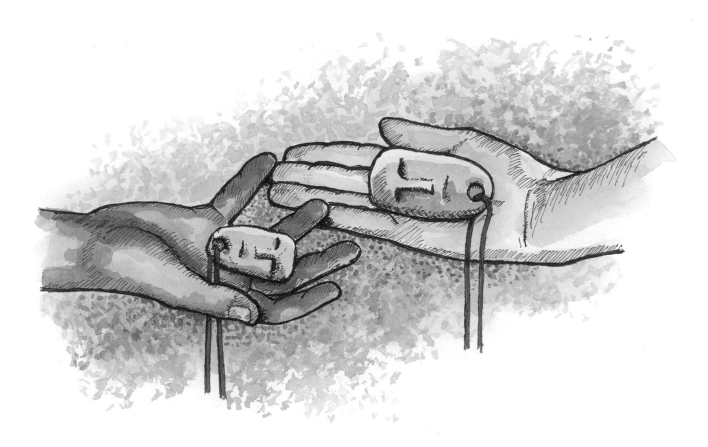

I was dumbstruck. Sarah was a complete stranger yet she was revealing her deepest secrets to me. The stone had indeed created a strong bond of trust between us.

"Finn, does your stone ever become warm?" she asked.

"Yes, a lot," I answered. "The first time I felt it was when we were going through Lehigh Water Gap. I saw eagles flying above the Blue Mountain and I believe they were talking to me.

"Then there was the time I was in a great forest near White Haven and lumberjacks were cutting enormous hemlock trees all around me. I couldn't stand to see them fall. I felt helpless and angry. It was like watching the forest's grandfathers being killed one by one.

"The worst time was in the gorge above Mauch Chunk. I saw a boat captain shoot a bear. The poor animal never suspected any trouble. It tumbled down the mountainside and the boat captain did nothing but laugh. My stone was red hot and I yelled at the captain until my father told me to stop. The next day the captain and his crew got sick from eating the meat."

Sarah smiled and reached for my hand.

"Finn, I am glad we met. I feel the spirit of Mesingw lives in both of us. I have witnessed acts of disrespect, too. And each time my stone becomes warm against my chest like yours.

"Lenapehocking is changing. Animals and forests are disappearing and the soil that supports all life is being lost to the winds and rivers. You and I understand the spirit of Mesingw, and because of that we will be friends forever. You and I respect the earth, and everything upon the earth."

A sense of calm came over me. The turtle reappeared on the log and gazed at Sarah and me. It had a look of wisdom.

"Sarah, do you hear the turtle talking?" I quietly asked my friend.

"Yes, Finn, I do," she said. "And do you?"

"Yes, I do. It's telling me to be patient and thoughtful and to always have courage."

I turned to thank Sarah for sharing her story but she was gone. I never saw her again. But the time she and I spent together on Gwinner's Island changed my life. Like the turtle, I learned great patience. And as time went on, my walks upon the earth became increasingly soft and gentle.

CHAPTER

23
ON TO NEW HOPE

We spent most of Sunday at St. Bernard's Church in Easton. Father learned a lot about the Delaware Canal by talking to other boat captains after the church service. They said it really wasn't much different than the Lehigh Canal. Locks were narrower and the lifts and drops not as high, but the general rules were the same and everybody moved cargo from place to place in the least amount of time.

We loaded the iron pigs at Glendon on Monday morning and also stopped in South Easton to pick up thirty bales of wool. Father was delivering it to a mill in New Hope that was supposedly three times larger than Mr. Shimer's fulling mill along Saucon Creek. I wondered how a mill could be that big.

Our entrance to the Delaware Canal was at Snufftown, a nickname for a community called Williamsport located where the Lehigh River flows into the Delaware River. It had a reputation as a hangout for fun-loving boat captains and raftsmen. Log rafting was big business on the Delaware River, mostly in spring when the river was high. I heard

some rafters floated all the way from the great Pocono Mountains to Philadelphia.

The Delaware Canal was supplied by Lehigh River water. The water entered the canal through a feeder channel that was part of a complicated lock system. There was a guard lock for entering and leaving, a weigh lock for weighing boats and cargo, and an outlet lock where boats could cross the Delaware River and enter the Morris Canal in Phillipsburg, New Jersey.

The Delaware River dominated the scenery no matter where we were. It was very broad – more than twice the width of the Lehigh – and looked quite deep. There were rapids and large boulders that must have been terrible obstacles for the rafters.

Conan and Rogan loved walking along a new canal. I borrowed Father's pocket watch and estimated our speed at about four miles an hour. We locked through double locks at Raubsville and entered Bucks County at Riegelsville. A short time later we passed a large iron works at Durham Furnace. Father said it was built in the early 1700s and that cannons and cannonballs for General Washington's army were made there.

The river made a big bend to the left in Kintnersville. Reddish cliffs called "The Palisades" rose sharply to the right of the canal. Somehow a wagon lane called River Road was squeezed between the canal and the cliffs. Boaters called this place "The Narrows." I could understand why.

The tall cliffs drew my attention as we towed through. I had never seen rocks rise up so straight before, nor had I seen any that were reddish in color. The cliffs were covered with moss and ferns and small shrubs. Water seeped from cracks in the rock and trickled to the bottom. I looked toward the top and saw an eagle lazily circling above the cliffs in search of a mid-day meal. It was the first eagle I had seen since Lehigh Water Gap.

Just ahead was Lock 20, which was recently rebuilt to hold two boats side-by-side. Father said the Pennsylvania government wasn't expecting a whole lot of traffic when they built the canal in 1832, so they built the locks to handle only one boat at a time. But they were wrong. Canal business boomed, and when the Lehigh Coal and Navigation Company bought the canal, one of the first things the owners did was widen some of the locks so two boats could get through. That way the canal could handle more boats and make more money.

The reddish cliffs became shorter after we passed The Narrows Hotel. They finally disappeared and the land flattened into long wide fields dotted with farms. I looked across the river to New Jersey and saw large stone quarries. They supplied limestone to make cement for the canal.

We passed underneath a hump-shaped bridge called a "camelback" and made a turn away from the river. This was new. Wherever I had been before, the canal followed the river. Now we were going inland. We didn't see the Delaware River again for seven miles. I sat on the bow of the boat and enjoyed the new view.

The quiet of the warm afternoon was suddenly pierced by a loud, high-pitched screech. I looked ahead of the boat and saw an eagle rising from the towpath with a rabbit in its sharp claws.

"Colin, did you see that?" I shouted.

"Yes!" he shouted back. "I saw him catch it, almost right in front of me."

The eagle rose higher. Then came a second cry. *"Screeeeee."*

"Finn, look, it lost a feather!" Colin yelled. "It's coming down toward the boat."

I saw it. Sure enough, it was floating right toward the *Belfast Queen*.

"Finn, try to catch it!" Colin urged.

That was exactly what I had in mind. But it was floating so slowly that I didn't know if I'd get a chance. I stood up on the front of the boat and steadied myself. To get the feather, I was ready to move in any direction except into the canal.

"Colin, slow down the mules! The feather is going to float over the boat if we don't slow down."

"Okay, I will. Tell me how much."

Until now Father had not said a word. But our slower speed put the *Belfast Queen* in a position of slowing down boats behind us, which their captains wouldn't like.

"Finn!" Father called. "I hope you catch the feather but I can't have Colin slow us down for too long."

"I understand, Father," I said. "I'll do my best."

"Colin, slow down just a little more!" I yelled.

The *Belfast Queen* slowed to a crawl. I looked up. The feather was still on course for the boat. I went as far front on the bow as possible and held my breath. Out of nowhere a little gust of wind whipped up and blew the feather right at me in tight little circles. I crouched low and then leaped, just catching the quill between my thumb and forefinger.

"You got it, Finn!" Colin shouted. "It was perfect!"

I stood on the deck, proudly examining my catch. It was a tail feather, broad and black except for a white band at the top.

"It will keep you from danger," a voice whispered.

Sarah!

My eyes darted to each side of the canal but no one was there. I didn't imagine those words, but who said them?

"Keep it with you always."

And that was the end. I never heard the voice again. But I was sure it was Sarah. From that moment, the feather stayed with me wherever I went.

"Colin!" Father shouted. "Put Conan and Rogan back to a normal walk."

"Yes, sir!"

And on we went, past Upper Black Eddy and Lodi and lots of farms. The narrow river road widened and was busy with wagons carrying hay and produce. Some wagons held mounds of round rocks from the Delaware River. Father said they were going to be used to make streets in Philadelphia. They must have been bumpy streets.

We arrived at a little village called Mexico that had so many buildings owned by a man named Uhler that it could have been called Uhlertown. We stayed in Mexico that night, which was not a popular decision with Colin and me. One of Mr. Uhler's buildings was a hay press. It made the neatest rectangular bales of hay I ever saw, but it had to be the noisiest machine on Earth. Because it was the peak of harvest season, the machine operated all night. Good gracious! Colin and I didn't get much more than forty winks.

We were happy to get out of Mexico the following morning. Father stopped to load some river rocks just down the canal at Erwinna. They were going with us to Bristol. While our boat was being loaded, I watched a new one being built at Erwinna's boatyard. I wondered if they'd paint it green. So far, the *Belfast Queen* was the only green boat I had seen in our travels.

The canal eventually turned back toward the Delaware River. It was fast and full of large islands. I saw the remains of a house on one of them; others had broken-down shacks. The biggest island had a sign in front of it that read "Marshall's Island." I wondered who Marshall was.

Colin liked his new shoes, but a ride on Conan's back was always a relief. Colin rode the mule a couple of miles to Point Pleasant before he had to jump down and walk the team over the Tohickon Creek aqueduct. Father said it was the longest on the canal.

We arrived next at Lumberville, where there were a lot of sawmills and stone quarries. There was also an old building called the Black Bass Hotel that sat right between the canal and the river road. We smelled food as we passed. Father's appetite must have been tweaked because we stopped and ate a tavern dinner. The food was delicious. I also enjoyed hearing a man tell stories about a gang of bandits called the Doanes.

"Boys, we have about five miles more until we reach New Hope," Father said. "It has been an eventful day, hasn't it?"

"Yes, Father," we both said. And indeed it had. A new canal, a new river, a new eagle feather.

Our stomachs full, we pulled away from the Black Bass Hotel – Colin aboard Conan, Father sitting at the front of the boat, and me leaning on the tiller and steering it. I had finally earned Father's trust to handle the *Belfast Queen*.

"Finn, we're coming up on New Hope!" Father shouted. "You take the boat into the basin."

"Yes, sir! Thank you, Father!"

Indeed, it had been a *very* good day.

CHAPTER

24

THE FINAL LEG

Owning a green boat had two advantages: Everyone could see it, and it attracted lots of curious people who wanted to know why Father chose such a bright color when all the other boats were kind of dull. I have a suspicion that was part of Father's plan from the beginning.

Wagon drivers found us wherever we docked, which was a good thing. Quick deliveries saved us time, and as Father reminded constantly, the more time we saved, the more profit we made.

But on this day in New Hope, Father's business connection was late, and he was growing impatient. The iron pigs and wool had been unloaded, but we were scheduled to deliver flour to Bristol and the wagons carrying it were nowhere in sight. If the flour wasn't loaded on our boat soon, we'd be forced to stay in New Hope overnight and lose a day's travel. Father scanned the road for the wagons, but his eyes also focused on his pocket watch. Finally, Father decided to take the situation into his own hands.

"Colin, Finn, come here please! I have an important job for you."

"Boys, I can't wait any longer. Please go find the wagons or the flour mill, whichever you see first. Ask the drivers to get here as quickly as possible."

"Yes, Father," Colin said. "But how do we get there?"

"You ride Rogan and Finn will take Conan," Father said. "The street in front of us is River Road. Follow it until you come to Phillips Mill."

Neither of us offered any ifs, ands or buts. A ride on the mules through a town? You bet! Father's plan would be followed to the letter. We unharnessed our friends and walked them toward the street.

People in New Hope were not accustomed to seeing mules wearing straw hats and cow bells on River Road. We received a lot of stares and a few laughs. Colin and I didn't care. Conan and Rogan were bigger than any horse on the street. It made us feel kind of important being a head taller than everyone.

We rode past Bridge Street and went north of town, keeping an eye open for a parade of wagons from Phillips Mill. They never appeared. We rode past farm after farm. I saw barns so big they could have held the *Belfast Queen* and two more just like it. We stopped at a spot where there was a clean line of sight, but we still couldn't see the wagons. The river was broad and quiet.

"Look at that covered bridge, Finn," Colin said, pointing back toward New Hope. "I never saw a bridge that long. Do you see the town on the other side?"

"I do, Colin, but let's not dawdle. We better keep riding and find Phillips Mill. Father is waiting for us."

Luckily, Phillips Mill was right around the next bend in the road. Even luckier was that seven big wagons had just pulled away from the mill and were heading toward us.

"Hello, sir!" Colin yelled to the first driver. "Our name is Gorman. Are you taking your load of flour to the *Belfast Queen*?"

"Why, yes, boy, we are," the man said. "We were told to look for a green boat. Is it true your boat is green?"

"Yes, sir, it's true," Colin replied, turning to me with a big grin. "We'll lead you to it."

We rode back to New Hope and were passing the Indian statue at the Logan Inn when Father spotted us. He broke into a smile and waved to get the attention of the lead wagon driver, but that wasn't necessary.

"Boy, there's your Pa's boat!" the driver shouted to me. "It's really green! Doggone, I guess the story *is* true."

The seven wagons picked their way through the busy street and stopped in front of the boat basin. With so much help, the sacks of flour were loaded in a little less than two hours. Father was pleased but still looked at his pocket watch more than usual.

"Let's be going!" he shouted when the last sack was loaded. "I'd like to get to Bristol before dark."

The Delaware River was very fast and dropped in elevation quickly at the southern end of New Hope. That meant the canal had to drop in elevation quickly, too. There were four locks built along a stretch of towpath that was less than half of a mile long. Boats dropped nearly thirty feet after locking through all of them.

Boat captains who wanted to cross the Delaware River to New Jersey could do that at New Hope. They exited the Delaware Canal through an outlet lock and were pulled across the river by wire cable to Lambertville, where they entered the Delaware and Raritan Canal. From there they could travel to Trenton, New Jersey's capital, or even up to New York. Now the list of canals I knew about was up to four.

South of New Hope, the Delaware River flattened into long quiet pools. Locks became less frequent and more distant from each other. Conan and Rogan settled into an easy four-mile-per-hour pace and Colin got some restful rides on their backs. I propped myself up against the water barrel and enjoyed the pleasant autumn scenery.

People who lived along the canal had tables set up with fresh fruits and vegetables, hoping to sell some to passing boats. With fifteen pennies from Father in my pocket, I vaulted to the towpath and bought a fresh chicken, three large potatoes, six carrots, and a loaf of freshly baked bread. The farmer's wife gave me some butter I couldn't afford to buy. Since this was the final leg of our journey down the Delaware Canal, I thought I'd prepare a special meal to celebrate.

Many buildings in Bucks County were very old. I saw a stone tower high atop a hill that looked like it was ready to crumble. It must have provided a great view of the entire river valley. Father heard that General Washington had soldiers climb up there to spy on British troops during the War for Independence. He thought we were close to the spot where General Washington crossed the Delaware River on Christmas Eve in 1776. I remembered reading about that in my history book at school.

The hours went by quickly. We passed a long rapids in the river at Yardley and dropped through three locks in less than two miles. Then we had a straight tow through land that became flatter and flatter as we traveled farther south.

The sun dipped and cast long shadows across the river. I looked at the still water and saw thousands of dimples on the surface that looked like rain drops. But it wasn't raining. I picked up Father's spyglass to get a closer look and saw a group of tiny silver fish break the water and leap into the air. Right behind them was a large fish with its mouth open. The closer I looked, the more dimples I saw. The river was full of the little fish, which I later learned were baby shad heading for the great Atlantic Ocean. The big fish was having a grand time catching an easy meal.

We passed a little town called Morrisville and turned away from the river as we had at Upper Black Eddy. The canal went through wide, flat marshland that smelled faintly of salt. The marshes were filled with long-legged white birds and thousands of squawking ducks and geese. It looked like the marsh water had been higher at one time, but now it was so low that it didn't even cover the roots of all the marsh plants.

"Colin!" Father shouted. "We'll be in Bristol soon. Listen for my directions when we get there."

We dropped through Lock 4 at Tullytown and entered Bristol less than thirty minutes later. The

Delaware River had returned. It must have been a half-mile wide and was full of all kinds of boats. There were ocean ships with tall straight masts and white sails, and other boats with smokestacks and silly looking paddlewheels. I saw canal boats tied together into large "rafts" that were being pulled downriver by steam-powered tugs. A hundred more canal boats were moored in a basin along the river's edge.

Warehouses filled with flour, corn, oats and rye lined the river's shoreline. I saw great coal yards and lumber piled twenty feet high. There were stacks of iron pigs and iron rails and slabs of granite. There were enough materials at Bristol to build a country.

"Father," I said. "Is this the end of our trip?"

"Just for today, Finn," he smiled. "We'll unload the flour tomorrow. Right now let's find a mooring spot for the night. Then we can have that special supper you promised."

The chicken was tender and the potatoes baked to perfection. I surprised everyone with an apple pie and brewed Father an especially good pot of coffee. It would be an hour until darkness and I had an itch to explore.

"Father, may I walk to the marsh?" I asked. "I won't stay long. Colin, would you like to come along?"

"Thanks, Finn, but my shoes need a rubbing with linseed oil. I'll see you when you get back."

"Be careful, Finn," Father said as I walked off the boat. "And don't get lost. I don't know how I'd replace you."

The marsh water had gotten deeper since the afternoon. The quacking of the ducks and geese was so loud I could barely hear myself think. I picked my way along the shoreline, watching the long-legged white birds stab fish with their slender, tapered beaks. When they caught one, they'd throw back their heads, open their mouths and gulp down the whole fish. I wondered how the prickly fins didn't get caught in the birds' throats.

Then I noticed a strange creature in the water. It was a little bigger than my hand, with an oval body colored greenish-blue. It had three short legs on each side of its body and two more legs in the front. The front legs ended in big, toothy pinchers. I had seen pinchers on crayfish in Saucon Creek, but they were nothing compared to these.

I thought for a moment. Then it dawned on me that I had seen a drawing of this critter in the *Moby Dick* book Colin borrowed from Mr. Nimsch. It was a blue crab. I thought I'd try to catch it.

I knelt down, closed my eyes, and took a deep breath before sticking my hand into the water. Then I opened my eyes and lowered my head toward the marsh's glassy surface. I looked for the crab but didn't see it. I looked again, but still no crab. Where had it gone?

I sensed something was oddly out of place. I looked at the shoreline and noticed the sand had disappeared. The smell of salt was gone, too. And where were the quacks and honks of the ducks and geese that serenaded me just moments ago?

Suddenly a loud whistle pierced the silence. I looked up, thinking it was a steamboat announcing itself on the Delaware River. But my eyes couldn't locate a steamboat or even the broad Delaware. Then the whistle blasted a second time. I looked into the distance and saw a cloud of steam and a sleek black locomotive pulling a string of railroad cars filled with coal. It was traveling along the bank of a strangely familiar river…not the Delaware, but another river I knew from somewhere before.

The train passed underneath an iron bridge that connected two small towns. I recognized many of the buildings and noticed an old stone-and-log home high on a hill across the river that had a friendly, inviting look. Where was I? What was happening to me?

I closed my eyes and resisted opening them. I realized I was returning to a life I hoped I could avoid, but I had no power to change things. I gathered enough strength to open my eyes and looked down toward my outstretched hands. They were full of wrinkles. Then I touched my mouth and felt a soft moustache above my lips. My fingers ran over loose, saggy cheeks. My heart sank. The marsh was gone, and so was the life of adventure I had lived the last two weeks. I was back in Freemansburg, kneeling alongside the Lehigh Canal where my excitement had begun. I was eighty-five years old once again.

I stared into the still green water, hoping for the impossible. But no matter how closely I looked, I could not see a single strand of bushy brown hair or even a small patch of smooth fair skin. My eyes had lost their sparkle and twinkle. I knew that my time of reliving my youth was over.

I slowly stood up and brushed the towpath dust off my rumpled trousers. Across the river was Shimersville and the hill where I discovered my Indian stone. I took a long look at the old stone-and-log home that rested there. I was sure I saw two mules running through the corn field behind it.

A bench along the towpath seemed to invite me to sit down, and I accepted the invitation. I spread an arm across the top of the bench and stretched my legs. They were tired and needed rest.

"It was a glorious time," I said out loud. "Good gracious, how I enjoyed it."

I tilted my head backward and slowly closed my eyes. In my mind I saw a deer standing underneath a hemlock tree and an eagle soaring through tall, white clouds. Sarah was watching a turtle bask in the afternoon sun. A black bear and its cubs waded in a river next to her. My family was gathered at the supper table, laughing at silly stories about Conan and Rogan. I saw myself hurdling down a mountain in a Switchback car, scared out of my wits yet enjoying every second of the ride.

And there, in the middle of all these wonderful memories was my Indian stone, glowing in a golden aura that radiated a comforting warmth and feeling of safety.

A sigh of relief left my body. My mind slowly drifted into a deep sleep, and I wondered where my next great adventure would take me.

THE END

AUTHOR & ILLUSTRATOR BIOGRAPHIES

Tales of the Towpath author, Dennis Scholl, is Director of Education for the Delaware & Lehigh National Heritage Corridor. He holds a Bachelor of Arts degree in History from The Pennsylvania State University and has worked as a staff writer and editor for the *Bethlehem-Globe Times* newspaper and Rodale Press magazines. Dennis also served as an elementary school environmental education consultant for nine years. He and his wife, Josephine, live in Hellertown, Northampton County.

Illustrator Dennis Gerhart graduated from the Philadelphia College of Art with a Bachelor of Science degree in Industrial Design. He has worked with architects and designers for more than thirty-five years. Dennis has a long interest in early Pennsylvania transportation and history and has produced numerous pen-and-ink drawings and watercolors. In addition to his work for *Tales of the Towpath*, Dennis has produced a series of drawings for displays along the Delaware Canal in New Hope. Dennis resides outside of Quakertown, Bucks County, with his wife Maria.

PROJECT SPONSORS

The *Tales of the Towpath* curriculum is made possible by funding from:

Pennsylvania Department of Conservation and Natural Resources

Lehigh Valley Community Foundation

J & K Hommer Foundation

Pennsylvania Department of Community and Economic Development,
through Senator Robert Wonderling

Keystone Nazareth Charitable Foundation

Embassy Bank

Sovereign Securities and Sovereign Bancorp

Capital Blue Cross

The Luzerne Foundation

Delaware & Lehigh National Heritage Corridor

NOTES

NOTES